A MISSING MOM AND MUTT MUNCHIES

LARGE PRINT EDITION

ALSO BY ALEKSA BAXTER

MAGGIE MAY AND MISS FANCYPANTS MYSTERIES

A Dead Man and Doggie Delights

A Crazy Cat Lady and Canine Crunchies

A Buried Body and Barkery Bites

A Missing Mom and Mutt Munchies

A Sabotaged Celebration and Salmon Snaps

A Poisoned Past and Puppermints

✷✷✷

A Fouled-Up Fourth

NOSY NEWFIE HOLIDAY SHORTS

Halloween at the Baker Valley Barkery & Cafe

A Housebound Holiday

A MISSING MOM
AND MUTT MUNCHIES

A MAGGIE MAAY AND MISS FANCYPANTS MYSTERY

ALEKSA BAXTER

Original Text Copyright © 2019 M.L. Humphrey
Large Print Edition © 2020 M.L. Humphrey
All Rights Reserved.
ISBN: 978-1-63744-012-4

CHAPTER 1

"Where's Fancy?" I asked my grandpa as I toweled my long blonde hair dry with one hand and rooted in the fridge for a Coke with the other. Normally when I took a shower she went to sleep at his feet, but he was seated at the kitchen table and there was no sign of Fancy anywhere.

He set aside his pen and half-completed crossword puzzle and reached for his non-existent cigarettes. (He'd stopped smoking when my grandma got sick, but lifelong habits don't die easy. He'd started smoking when he was twelve so that made close to seventy years of reaching for that pack of cigarettes tucked away in the breast pocket of his tried and true flannel shirt.)

"Where do you think, Maggie May?" He nodded towards the hallway that led to the backyard.

I sighed. "Bunnies."

"Rabbits. And wouldn't be a problem if you'd let me take care of 'em."

"You are not going to shoot a bunch of bunnies, Grandpa. One, because the neighbors would probably call the cops on you for using a gun in your backyard. Two, because even if they didn't, the police station is only a few blocks away and there's at least one cop there who would love to throw you in jail. And, three, because they're bunnies. Who shoots bunnies?"

"A homeowner who wants to protect the foundation of his house from varmint, that's who." He leaned back in his chair and glared me down.

I crossed my arms and glared right back at him. "They are not varmint. They're bunnies."

"They're rabbits. And where there are two rabbits there are ten and then a hundred."

A Missing Mom and Mutt Munchies

"We are not going to have a hundred rabbits. There are what, two, living back there?"

"More than that." He took a long sip of coffee, still glaring at me.

I just shook my head. "They're bunnies, Grandpa. No shooting, poisoning, or otherwise harming them."

As I made my way towards the backyard I wondered what I'd done in my thirty-six years of life to warrant my current situation—living with my eighty-two-year-old grandpa who most definitely did not feel a need for me to take care of him (although his predilection for using guns when he shouldn't indicated maybe he was wrong about that), running a not-yet-successful café and barkery in a small Colorado tourist town with my best friend (who had decided it was the perfect time to fall in love and get married), and trying to keep my precocious three-year-old Newfoundland, Miss Fancypants, from inadvertently killing a bunny in her desire to "play" with it.

This was nothing like the life I'd had just a few months before in

Aleksa Baxter

Washington, DC. And even though it was one I'd chosen for myself, it wasn't exactly peaches and cream.

Was it too much to ask that my grandpa actually need my help, that my business actually thrive, that my best friend not go and get all moony over some guy, and that my sweet-natured dog not turn into a stone-cold bunny killer?

I mean, honestly.

I stepped out on the back porch and spared a moment to admire the clear blue sky and the mountain covered in evergreens and aspen tress that rose behind my grandpa's house—a view worth all the frustrations in the world. But I didn't take too deep a breath. That time of year there was a yellow-flowered weed of some sort that grew all around and smelled decidedly musky.

Fancy was stationed on the bottom section of the ramp that led off the porch, her one hundred and forty pounds of furry bulk squeezed across the space over the last two slats. She was crammed in there so tight I wasn't sure how she was going to manage to stand back up.

A Missing Mom and Mutt Munchies

She looked up with a "please help me" look and a small whine before returning to licking the slats and snuffling at the space between them.

I sighed. "Fancy..."

I could never decide whether she was licking the slats because she wanted to make friends with the little furry creatures hiding underneath, or because she wanted to eat them. I'm honestly not sure she knew.

Whichever it was, I was just glad they were separated from her by two slats of very sturdy Trex decking. And glad, too, that my grandpa hadn't used wood to build the ramp or we'd be making frequent emergency trips to the vet to have splinters removed from Fancy's tongue.

I'd tried putting a welcome mat over the end of the ramp but she just pawed it away so she could get closer to the bunnies.

I was about to shove Fancy off the bottom of the ramp and tell her to go play in the yard and "leave it"—a command she usually obeyed—when I looked past her.

Aleksa Baxter

There in the grass, hunkered down not a foot away from Fancy, was a tiny little bunny about the size of my closed fist. It met my eyes and hunched its shoulders, pressing itself closer to the ground, not even smart enough to run away when it should.

I laughed. Once.

I know. I'm horrible, but I couldn't help it. There Fancy was, frantically licking at the slats on the ramp, crying her head off as she tried to get to the bunnies underneath it, and right behind her was one of the very bunnies she was looking for.

Fancy looked at me again and cried, pawing at the slats with both feet like she could somehow dig through the decking.

"Treat?" I said, hoping to lure her inside.

Her head tilted a bit at the magic word but then she went back to snuffling at the spot between the slats. Seemed there was something Fancy liked more than food. Who knew?

"I bet there isn't even a bunny under there, you big goof." I sat

A Missing Mom and Mutt Munchies

down next to her and peered between the slats, expecting to see nothing, but right there on the far right side was just a hint of brindled fur. So two bunnies. At least. Seemed my grandpa was right.

(And I should mention here that I call all rabbits bunnies. It's a quirk I have. To me rabbits belong on a fancy dinner menu at some four-star restaurant. Bunnies are the cute little things that infest your yard with their furry white tails and complete lack of survival skills.)

I stood up. "Come on, Fancy. Let's go inside."

She didn't budge.

Since she doesn't wear a collar at home I grabbed her by the ruff of her neck and tried to pull her towards the door. She cried out like I was torturing her and rolled onto her back.

Which was not an act of surrender, I might add, although it might look like it to the uninitiated. Oh no, Fancy and her rolling on her back because she doesn't want to go somewhere is straight out of the pacifist playbook.

It's like she's saying, "Look, I'm showing you my belly and making it so you can't actually get ahold of me to move me anywhere. Why don't you just give up on what you had planned and pet me instead?"

Normally at that point I would've started a countdown because I was not about to fall for that one, but unfortunately the foolish little bunny that had decided to hang out a foot from a very large predator chose that moment to make a run for it.

Away from the ramp.

Fancy scrambled to her feet and chased after it while I chased after her shouting "Leave it" as loud as I could—a command that had absolutely no effect on Fancy because there was a small scurrying thing running along the ground and she was no longer an overweight domesticated house pet but instead a descendent of wolves who needed to catch her prey or else risk starving to death.

Fortunately, the bunny somehow managed to dart past Fancy—baby bunnies are really fast—and through the slats in the deck. At which point

A Missing Mom and Mutt Munchies

Fancy started very loudly voicing her opinion about being defeated in her efforts to eat a bunny by crying at the top of her lungs.

My grandpa poked his head out the door. "What happened?"

"She chased a bunny under the porch." I tried to push her towards the house, but she dug in and wouldn't budge.

He opened the door wider. "Fancy. Here. Now."

Fancy hesitated for half a second, but no one refuses my grandpa when he uses that particular tone of voice. She slunk up the ramp, glancing back at me once before going inside.

"That was far too close," I told my grandpa.

"You need to let me take care of 'em. One of these days she'll get ahold of one and then what will you do?"

I didn't even want to think about that. I knew she wouldn't kill one on purpose, but you take a tiny bunny and a big dog and put the one in the other's mouth and it's not going to come out well.

Aleksa Baxter

My life. I swear. Why couldn't it be simple and perfect? Was that really too much to ask?

CHAPTER 2

I followed my grandpa into the kitchen for breakfast. For some reason I'd decided I was getting old and losing my mind so I'd started trying to eat healthier, which meant breakfast consisted of oats soaked in yogurt with blueberries, bananas, shredded coconut, and some cinnamon sprinkled on top.

It wasn't bad, but it wasn't the bacon and eggs I wanted.

(And, yes, there was still a Coke involved. I am quite well aware of my hypocrisy, thank you very much. I figure baby steps are better than no steps at all.)

"So what are you up to today?" I asked him. "Lesley coming over?"

He shook his head. "Her husband's in hospice. I don't expect I'll see her until he passes."

"Oh, Grandpa, I'm sorry."

He and Lesley had an awkward situation. They'd once dated and been in love, but then he'd been sent away to prison for killing her sister's abusive husband. While he was gone she'd met her current husband and married him. (With my grandpa's blessing. He'd thought he'd be in a lot longer than he was.)

It had all worked out in the end. Lesley's husband was a good man. He'd even given my grandpa a job when he got out of prison for the second time, and my grandpa had ended up with my grandma and been happily married for forty years until she died of cancer.

But since then he and Lesley had spent a lot of time together because her husband was in the end stages of Parkinson's and she needed to get away sometimes. Being a caretaker is not easy.

Nothing had happened between them as far as I knew, but there was

A Missing Mom and Mutt Munchies

definitely a more than friends vibe to what they had. Which meant staying away from Lesley had to be killing my grandpa.

But even worse was probably trying to figure out what happened next. Small towns are not always forgiving when you cross the invisible lines of propriety. And since their special friendship was well-known after the Jack Dunner incident, all eyes would be on them, watching and judging.

My grandpa shrugged it away. "Lesley's the one you should be sorry for, not me. But because she's taking care of Bill I'm stuck making twelve dozen cookies for the end of season baseball party."

"End of season? So soon?"

He nodded. "House will be full of pretty much everyone in town Saturday when we have the big end of season awards and pot luck."

(Not that that was a lot of people. Creek only has about forty homes total.)

I wanted to ask him if Matt had said anything more about whether he was going to stick around or not, but I didn't dare. My grandpa would read way too much into my question. Honestly. Just because I asked a question about a guy did not mean that I was in love with him and desperate to know if he was going to re-enlist or not.

(Even though I was. Not that I was going to let Matt or anyone else know. And if they did figure it out that didn't mean I was going to act on it. There were reasons I was single. Reasons with a capital R. And being in love with a gorgeous, decent, intelligent man didn't change any of them.)

My grandpa glared at his crossword puzzle and set it aside half-finished. "I also have to mow the yard and weed out that plot on the north side of the house. What are you up to on your day off?"

I grimaced. "I was planning on reading a book. My favorite author just released the final book in her latest series, so I figured I'd spend the day devouring it."

I'd really wanted to read that book, too. There's nothing I love more than getting lost in a good story. But...

A Missing Mom and Mutt Munchies

"I don't need to, though," I added. "I'll mow the yard for you instead."

"Mow the yard? Why would I let you do that?"

"Because it's hot out and you're..."

"Old?" He shook his head. "I may be eighty-two-years-old but I am perfectly capable of mowing my own yard." (There was an extra word in there before yard that I'm not including here. My grandpa doesn't mince words and doesn't appreciate having anyone question his health or stamina.)

"I'm just saying, Grandpa. I'm here. Use me. I moved in with you to help out around here. And mowing the yard is part of that."

Ever since I'd moved in I'd been feeling like a burden more than a help. Half of the reason I'd moved to Creek was so he'd have someone to take care of him, but he wouldn't let me.

He snorted. "You want to help out?"

"Yes. Please."

"Fine. You can bake the cookies. Here's the recipe. Ingredients are in

15

the fridge." He slid a piece of paper across the table.

Walked right into that one, hadn't I?

I sighed. The last thing I wanted to do on my day off from working at a bakery was to bake. But I wasn't about to say no and my grandpa knew it. "Great. Love to. I'll get right on that after I finish breakfast."

My grandpa winked at me before picking his crossword puzzle back up with a smug little smile.

CHAPTER 3

Twenty minutes later, with Fancy out back on alert for bunnies and my grandpa out front mowing the yard, I stared at my grandpa's kitchen, hands on hips, prepared to do battle with an ancient oven and warped cookie trays. All for a bunch of kids that weren't even mine or related to me in any way.

What had my life become?

But when my grandpa actually voiced a need for my help, I wasn't going to turn him down, so there was no turning back.

I grabbed my phone, started Rebecca Ferguson playing, cranked up the volume, and went to work.

I do actually like to bake. I find it relaxing, especially when I have good music playing in the background. It's just when I'm forced to do so that I get a little cranky.

But within minutes I'd settled into my rhythm and was happily singing about how nothing's real but love (ironic, I know, given my own aversion to the feeling) while I mixed my ingredients and pre-heated the oven.

I'd just finished stirring in the chocolate chips when I turned to find Matt standing in the doorway, grinning at me. He wasn't in uniform but was instead wearing a pair of well-fitting and well-worn jeans with a blue t-shirt that matched his eyes.

Honestly, it's not fair for a man to look as good as he does without even trying. Check the dictionary under tall, dark, and handsome and you'd probably find a picture of him.

Not that I cared. I was too busy coughing my head off because I'd stopped singing so abruptly I almost choked myself to death.

"Need some water?" he asked, still smiling at me.

"I don't drink water." I grabbed a Coke from the fridge and took a deep

A Missing Mom and Mutt Munchies

gulp. "How long were you standing there?"

"Long enough to hear you make it through a song or two."

"Seriously?" I could've melted into the floor right then. I love to sing but I try not to torture others with it. I've been told nails on a chalkboard sound better. "I'm sorry. Why didn't you say anything? I would've stopped."

"Why would I want to stop you?"

"Because I'm horrible."

He shrugged. "A little off-key, but I didn't mind. It's not often I see you so relaxed and happy." He grabbed himself a Coke and sat down at the kitchen table as he cracked it open. "Where's Fancy?"

"Out back. She's developed an obsession with bunnies."

"That's not going to end well."

"Tell me about it." I started scooping cookie dough onto the cookie sheet, needing something to do so I wouldn't start thinking about those poor bunnies.

Matt came over and snagged a bit of cookie dough. "Mm. That's good. What are you baking for?"

"Your team as it turns out. My grandpa guilted me into doing it since Lesley can't."

"Ah, yeah. Sad news about Bill. He's had a rough time of it the last month or so."

"Do you know everyone in this town?" I'd visited in the summers, but hadn't grown up in the Baker Valley. Matt had, though. And now he was a police officer which probably put him in contact with even more people.

"Not everyone. Just the troublemakers, like you, and family friends, like Bill and Lesley. Bill was best friends with my grandpa. Spent a decent amount of time around him when I was growing up. Good man."

"Small towns, I swear. There's, what, three degrees of separation between any two people here?"

"More like one."

He reached for another taste of cookie dough and I slapped at his

A Missing Mom and Mutt Munchies

hand. "Take a beater if you're going to keep eating my cookie dough."

"Yes, ma'am."

As he helped himself to one of the beaters and started to lick it clean—something I tried very hard not to pay attention to—I put the first cookie tray in the oven. "Why are you out of uniform anyway? Thought you worked today."

He grimaced and sat back down at the kitchen table, stretching his legs out. "I decided to take a little time off. Lots of decisions to make now that the baseball season is wrapping up."

Suddenly my throat felt too dry. I grabbed my Coke and took a nice long swallow. "What kind of decisions?"

He leaned against the wall. "Jack's decided to stick around for a bit. Said he wants to get on the straight and narrow. Asked if he could crash with me while he does. Figured I can't say no since it's our dad's place."

That sounded like a non-answer, but it wasn't. One of the things Matt struggled with most as a small-town cop was the fact that he had to arrest or investigate his friends and family. And since his brother Jack was a criminal to the core—a good-looking, fun-loving, not going to hurt someone if he could steal their television while they were out sort of criminal, but a criminal nonetheless—his deciding to stick around town meant Matt was probably going to have to arrest him at some point.

Not to mention Jack's bizarre statement that when he was healed up he was going to make a pass at me, something that Matt most definitely hadn't been happy about. (Even though he'd yet to make a real pass at me himself.)

"Okay. So you're just taking a couple weeks off so you won't have to be the one to arrest Jack when he changes his mind?"

"That's part of it."

I grabbed the other beater so I'd have an excuse not to look at him as I asked, "And the other part of it?"

"I got a re-enlistment offer. It's a pretty good one."

A Missing Mom and Mutt Munchies

I turned to stare at him, wanting so much to tell him to tear it up and throw it in the trash. But I couldn't. That wasn't fair to him. I couldn't ask him to make that decision for me when I knew I wasn't going to be there for him if he did.

I forced myself to sound casual as I asked, "You think you'll take it?"

He held my gaze for a few seconds more than was comfortable until I turned away to wipe down the counter. I'm the type of cook that can get flour on the ceiling, so there was a lot to wipe down.

"I'm considering it," he said.

I gotta tell you, I hate conversations with subtext to them. There he was, sitting in my kitchen, basically telling me he was going to leave and re-enlist in the military and what he was really doing was asking me if I wanted him to stay, poking around at the edges trying to figure out if there was some sort of a possibility of there being an "us" at some point.

We both knew that's what he was doing, but neither one of us was going to come at the issue head on. Heaven forbid.

Of course, that's what **I** figured was going on. There was always the chance that his interest in me was all in my head and I was just making up feelings that weren't there. I swear, I have spent far too many moments of my life trying to figure out if there's anything happening below the surface of a conversation when nine times out of ten there probably isn't.

Most people are not as complex as I give them credit for.

But with Matt...

It didn't matter. I couldn't tell him what he wanted to hear from me. Matt was pretty much the perfect guy. Good-looking, good-hearted, smart, and with that undefinable something that drew me in. But relationships...

They're just not my thing.

Especially since I'd been forced to watch my best friend and business partner Jamie act like a lovesick fool the last couple of weeks. Honestly, I swear, if it was possible to float from happiness she would've been. And

A Missing Mom and Mutt Munchies

that kind of giddy, out-of-control foolishness was not what I wanted. Not at all.

But I didn't want him to go either.

"You're a good cop, you know. This town needs you."

"You really think so?"

Before I could answer, my grandpa stomped into the kitchen. "Maggie, you burn those cookies you're not going to do any of us any good."

I whirled around to check on the cookies and by the time I was done getting them out of the oven and onto a cooling rack Matt and my grandpa had disappeared out back to have a talk. I desperately wanted to know what my grandpa's advice was going to be, but instead I busied myself with getting the next cookie tray ready and in the oven.

I swear, life was a lot simpler when I was just a self-absorbed workaholic who lived alone and had no romantic prospects.

CHAPTER 4

That Saturday I actually managed to attend the final baseball game of the Creek Coyotes, the town baseball team that my grandpa coached and that Matt had been helping out with most of the season. Normally I would've been working, but Jamie told me to take the afternoon off—we weren't exactly slammed with business even on a Saturday afternoon.

Putting aside thoughts of destitution and bad life choices, I settled Fancy and myself in a spot of shade along the first baseline.

I loved the baseball field in Creek. The whole town was surrounded by mountain ranges that thrust into a clear blue sky and the grass was brilliantly green, which for the

A Missing Mom and Mutt Munchies

mountains wasn't always the case. There's far more scrub brush than grass the higher up you go. But the town prided itself on its ball field.

There were even cute little white-washed dugouts for each of the teams, something that hadn't existed when I was a kid. And two sets of wooden bleachers painted a bright blue.

It was like an image straight out of a post card of small town America.

Fancy and I hadn't been there two minutes before Jack Barnes, Matt's older brother, came to join us.

Jack's trouble through and through. Setting aside his criminal proclivities, he's also the type of guy to make a woman lose all sense of reason and rationality. He's got the same tall, dark-haired, blue-eyed good looks as Matt, but he also has a mischievous streak a mile wide. One grin and suddenly running away to Cabo for the weekend to pick up a package for a friend starts to sound like a fun adventure instead of the life-threatening criminal enterprise it is.

27

"Maggie May Carver. To what do we owe the pleasure?" he asked as he settled in next to me.

Fancy rolled on her back as soon as he came close and Jack obliged by giving her a thorough tummy rub. (She's such a sellout it's ridiculous.)

"Figured I baked all the cookies for the end of year party, least I could do is make it to a game." Before he could make some smart comment about my cookies, I added, "And what brings you out?"

"Didn't you hear? I've decided to become a fine upstanding member of society. Means I have to interact with people and let them see how I've changed. Can't do that at the Creek Inn. Plus, I figured I could show my brother a little support."

"He said you're going to be living with him."

"I am. Which is going to make things really awkward when you and I get all hot and heavy." He leaned close enough he was almost touching me, but I wasn't looking at him. I was watching Matt watching us from the dugout, his hands fisted at his

A Missing Mom and Mutt Munchies

sides—until my grandpa whapped him in the back of the head, that is.

I glared at Jack. "You're not a very nice person, you know that?"

He leaned back on his elbows with a chuckle. "How so?"

"Matt's right over there. He can't do anything about it. And yet here you are hitting on me when you know..."

"What do I know, Maggie? That you pretended you guys were dating when I first met you. That doesn't make you off limits."

"You know that he..." I pressed my lips together.

"That he actually likes you? Hm. Seems you do, too." He leveled a look at me that reminded me of Matt's pin-you-to-the-wall interrogation stare. "So why are you playing my brother?"

"I'm not playing him. I just..." I shook my head. "Tell me you've never liked someone you **knew** you'd be no good for. It has to have happened to you."

"Never stopped me, though." He winked.

"Yeah, well, that's where we differ."

"So that's why you're keeping him at arms' length? Because you think you'd be bad for him? Why do you think that?"

Who knows where that conversation would've gone from there—nowhere good, that's for sure—but right then the kid playing first base—a small boy with red hair peeking out under his baseball cap and more freckles than any single person should ever have—missed a simple grounder when it ricocheted off his glove.

The other team erupted into cheering as the kid chased after the ball, and the batter, who'd thought he was out, continued on towards second.

The poor kid had to scramble under a car to get the ball. By the time he threw it back to the catcher what should have been a simple out had turned into a triple and the kid was crying his eyes out.

That would've been bad enough. But then a large hulking man in a stained white t-shirt, ratty jeans, and

A Missing Mom and Mutt Munchies

steel-toed boots stumbled over to the kid and started to scream at him. We were close enough to catch the reek of alcohol and body odor. A lovely combination, let me tell you.

"What was that?" the man shouted, looming over the poor kid. "And why are you crying? Man up. You've got a game to win."

The poor kid crouched into himself as if expecting a blow.

The dude was a good six inches taller than me, probably twice my weight, and muscled in a way I most definitely am not. Plus, something told me he didn't have qualms against hitting women, but I was about to get up and give him a piece of my mind.

Fortunately, Fancy beat me to it. She started barking her head off at him and even lunged in his direction.

By the time I got her under control, Jack was on his feet ready to throw a punch. That wouldn't have helped his new plans to become a good law-abiding citizen but before anything else could happen Matt, my grandpa, and the other team's head coach all converged on us.

So did a skinny woman with bright red hair and freckles to match the kid's. She grabbed at the man's arm "Come on, babe. Let's go home. Sam can get a ride after the party. Come on, baby. Let it go."

He shook her off. The way she flinched I was pretty sure that in another time and place he wouldn't have just shook her off, but hit her.

She didn't give up, though. She grabbed at him a second time and leaned into him, urging him to come away with her, murmuring something in his ear that finally had him calming down and stepping back.

We all watched them go, Matt with his hand on his cellphone. "I swear, he gets in that truck of his, I'm calling it in," he muttered.

But they didn't get in a vehicle. Just stumbled down the road towards a small set of rundown trailer homes a few blocks away.

Too bad. That was one man who deserved to be locked away from others from the little I'd seen.

A Missing Mom and Mutt Munchies

Surprisingly, it was Jack who led the boy away towards right field, leaning close to whisper to him as my grandpa, Matt, and the other coach got back to the business of playing small town baseball.

Jack knelt down to talk to the kid, gently wiping away his tears. Who knew he had that side to him? Within moments he had the kid calmed down and smiling. Not bad for a grifter and drifter.

As they made their way back towards us, I showered Fancy with a bunch of kisses and ear scratches because she was still a little wound up. "Good girl, Fancy. Way to bark at the bad man."

Jack nudged the kid back towards his dugout and dropped down next to me. "You going to give me a bunch of smooches and caresses, too, because I stood up to the bad man?"

I smacked him on the arm.

Hard.

He just grinned back at me and winked.

Men. I swear.

CHAPTER 5

The end of year party was a madhouse. Take a bunch of sugar-hyped kids that had just won their final game of the season and add all of their parents and their parents' friends and you have loud, crowded, and insane. Exactly the type of situation I wanted to avoid at all costs.

Normally, I would've used Fancy as an excuse and locked both of us away in my room until everyone was gone, but she was still on bunny watch. So while the kids ran through the house and filled up the front lawn she was out back stationed in the middle of the yard staring at the spot where that baby bunny had fled under the porch.

A Missing Mom and Mutt Munchies

I leaned against the railing. "Fancy, would you give it a rest?"

She didn't even look at me. All else had failed to exist for her except for those stupid bunnies.

Matt came out to join me. "Your grandpa said I might find you out here. She still looking for bunnies?"

"Unfortunately. I don't know what she's going to do if she actually manages to catch one. Why is it that we make dog toys look so much like animals?"

He grinned at me. "Because that's what they like to chew on. Buck, the dog we had when I was growing up, was a great birding dog. He'd retrieve those things like no one's business."

I stared at him. "Why are you telling me this? Why are you okay with that? I want a dog that lays on her bed, snores funny, and eats bon bons. Not a…bunny killer."

He just laughed. "Be glad you don't have a cat. They can climb trees. And get under decks like this one."

I shuddered at the thought. "So why are you out here with me instead of in there celebrating with the kids?"

"We just finished giving out all the awards so my part's done. And it just didn't seem right to leave you alone out here. Who knows who might corner you."

Ah, so that was it. He was keeping me company so Jack wouldn't. I did not need to be stuck between those two. But saying anything about it meant walking on very thin ice. So I chugged down the rest of my beer and shook the empty can. "I need another beer. Want one?"

"Sure."

Matt and I made our way out front to grab a couple cans of Coors from a big metal vat filled with ice. I let him play the gentleman because no way was I putting my hand in water that cold if I didn't have to. As he dug around for two cans of beer under all that ice I glanced over to the side of the house where Jack and the little boy from the game, Sam, were sitting off to the side talking.

"That's odd, isn't it?" I asked as Matt handed me my beer. "I never

A Missing Mom and Mutt Munchies

thought of Jack as being good with kids."

He followed the direction of my gaze. "Not really. Jack dated Trish last time he was around this way. Sam would've been maybe four or five at the time? Not sure how things were between Jack and Trish—she's a volatile one—but I know Jack really got a kick out of spending time with Sam. Bought him his first baseball glove."

"Really? I would've never guessed."

Matt took a long swig of his beer. "That's my brother. A man of hidden depths."

Of course, Jack chose that moment to wink at a woman I happened to know was very much married. I turned away, shaking my head. He was going to get himself shot (again) if he wasn't careful.

Three boys ran by us screaming at the top of their lungs and I winced. "I'm going inside and hiding from all this mess."

I wanted to just flee, alone, but I remembered how Matt had saved me at the charity thing so instead I added, "I guess you could come along if you want. I'm just going to be in my room listening to music."

He glanced around. "Alright. Sure. Sounds fun."

🐾 🐾 🐾

Matt and I spent the next two hours in my room listening to various songs and discussing our favorite music, me sprawled on the bed, him sprawled on the floor.

I felt like I was in high school again. Not that I'd ever actually had guys over to the house in high school. I'm not sure if it was a rule that they couldn't come over or if it just never happened. (Knowing me, it probably just never happened. Are you really surprised?)

All the same. It felt very high school. All that was missing was me wearing my hair in a high ponytail and chewing some form of fruity bubble gum while my parental unit checked that everything was "okay" every fifteen minutes.

We even left the bedroom door open so no one would think anything hinky was going on. Last thing I

A Missing Mom and Mutt Munchies

needed was to be the subject of small town gossip.

It was fun, though. Matt was definitely one of those rare guys I could spend hours with without getting bored or annoyed.

But eventually everyone headed out and so did he.

CHAPTER 6

The next morning I found myself in a battle of wills with Fancy. Normally I take her into work with me, but that morning she was having none of it. I went out back when it was time to go and she actually ran away from me.

"Fancy, what are you doing?"

She glanced towards the ramp where the bunnies were hiding and cried her little head off at me. She may not speak English but it was perfectly clear she did not want to have to abandon her bunny watch post.

"No. Leave it. Come on." If I let her stay home she'd sit there all day even when it was far too hot for her to be outside. Not to mention the chances of her actually snagging one,

A Missing Mom and Mutt Munchies

something I did not want to have happen.

I cornered her on the far side of the yard, but then she pulled her rolling on her back act. Even a nudge with my foot wasn't enough to get her to flip back over.

"Fancy, you have ten seconds." I stood over her and glared as I started my countdown. "Ten. Nine."

She wiggled and cried and rolled around on the ground like I was performing some sort of exorcism on her as I continued to count down towards one.

When I reached three I paused to glare at her. Was she really going to push it this time? If so, I wasn't quite sure what I'd do. Wrestling a collar onto her would probably be a lot like trying to wrestle a bear. Not a good idea.

"Two," I continued, as I leaned down. "One."

She cried one last time and then jumped to her feet. "Thank you." I put her collar on her before she ran away again. "Come on. We're going to be late."

She strained towards the ramp as we walked by, but at least she followed me back inside and out to the van.

As you can imagine, not being a morning person and then having to fight my dog to take her into work with me—something that she should have seen as a privilege and not a punishment—I was not in the best of moods when I finally pulled up outside the Baker Valley Barkery and Café, the business I ran with my best friend Jamie.

Which meant as I stared at the cute little sign with the barely-legible script and Newfie heads on either end that I wasn't feeling all that positive about things.

It had seemed like such a good idea when we came up with it. Part café for people—that was Jamie's side—and part bakery for dogs—that was my side. (Barkery. Get it? Haha.) What could be better than running a business with my best friend, living in a small town, and finally getting away from corporate life?

(Money, as it turns out. A steady paycheck is actually a nice thing to

A Missing Mom and Mutt Munchies

have. When you work for some large soulless corporation those paychecks come nice and steady, but when you're running your own place sometimes those paychecks don't come at all.)

It wasn't all bad. Jamie's cinnamon rolls had been a definite hit. And I did well with online sales at least. And I did have some regular customers—Greta and her Irish Wolfhound, Hans—but I was scared. Scared that I wasn't pulling my weight—Jamie could've probably run the café without the barkery and made twice as much. And also scared that now that she'd met Mason she wouldn't want to be there anymore. What would I do then?

I'd started a "Name the Treat" fundraiser for the local boys and girls club, figuring it would be a good way to get word out about the barkery and garner us some goodwill at the same time, but unfortunately I'd only had a grand total of five dollars donated in the first week and the names they'd suggested were just plain awful.

(One person had literally suggested "dog treats" as the name for my newest dog treat. Yeah, no.)

Take it from me. Never, ever, ever let strangers name your product.

Anyway. As I walked in the door I was already having a bad morning. Even the delicious smells of coffee and cinnamon rolls didn't help.

Nor did seeing Jamie singing to herself like some scene out of Snow White, her long brown braid swinging happily back and forth with each step she took as she cleaned the tables.

It got worse when I saw the paper.

It was just the **Baker Valley Gazette**, the local paper, so not like the statewide paper or anything, but still. The headline on the front page was **Local Police Too Incompetent To Solve Murders On Their Own**. And right below that, as part of the article, was a picture of yours truly.

I snatched the paper off the table and started reading as Jamie waved to me. "Hey, Maggie. Want a chocolate croissant? I think I've perfected the recipe."

A Missing Mom and Mutt Munchies

"Better make it two. And can you bring me a Coke?"

I didn't even bother to put Fancy in her cubby in the back of the barkery, just sat down at the nearest table and devoured the article.

It seemed that Peter Nielsen had gotten wind of the fact that I was involved with solving the last few murders in town. Rather than applaud me as a Good Samaritan helping out a hard-working police force (which was the truth) he'd used it as an opportunity to question their competence while painting me as an interfering busybody.

Jamie set a Coke and a plate with a delectable-looking chocolate croissant on the table in front of me. "Hi, Fancy girl. How are you this fine morning?" She gave Fancy a kiss on the nose and a good ear scratch while I finished the article.

I threw it aside and glared at the plate. "I thought I said two croissants?"

"You did. But part of being your best friend is knowing when you

45

mean something and when you don't. You'll be fine with one."

No I wouldn't.

But she was so darned happy I didn't have the heart to argue with her. Instead I took a bite of croissant. For a moment all my worries and anger disappeared, replaced by the sheer heaven of flaky, buttery pastry dough and real chocolate.

"Mmm. Delicious. You nailed it. This could've come straight from a street vendor in Paris."

"Thanks. Mason's mom helped me with the last little bit. She attended the Sorbonne when she was younger and still keeps a pied-à-terre in central Paris that she said Mason and I can borrow anytime we want. Wouldn't that be amazing? To live in Paris for like six months?"

I was surprised she didn't float out of her chair out of sheer happiness, which is why I didn't point out to her that living in Paris for six months would make it a little challenging to run the café on a daily basis.

Instead I said, "So you're getting on with the family, too, huh?"

A Missing Mom and Mutt Munchies

"Oh, absolutely. They're all wonderful."

Call me jaded (I am), but I figured they probably weren't all wonderful all the time. But love will do that to you. It's why it's best avoided like the plague. Clouds the senses.

"So you saw the article?" Jamie asked, sitting down across from me.

"Yeah. Doesn't paint a very flattering picture does it? Of any of us."

"I don't know. Depends on how you choose to see it. I think it's pretty impressive really that someone with no investigative training at all has been such a help to the police force."

I laughed. "You would see it that way, wouldn't you? I bet Matt won't. And I bet his boss won't either." I took a long sip of Coke and another bite of croissant to steady myself. "Well, it doesn't matter. Because I am not going to get involved in any other police matter ever. I swear, if I see another dead body I'm stepping over it and going on my merry little way. Let someone else deal with that mess. And if I get accused of murder again, I'll just confess and do the time."

"Mmhm. Sure you will." She gave me that knowing look she has.

"What does that mean?"

"It means I know you, Maggie. And if something else comes up and you think there's a way you can help, you're going to do it. You're not the type to turn away. And, heaven help the police if you think they're not doing a good job."

I lifted my chin in disagreement. "You're wrong. From this day forward I am keeping my nose in my own business."

Not even Fancy was buying it. She gave me a skeptical look from where she'd sprawled at my feet.

Jamie just laughed. "If you say so. Hey, when you're done here I need some help in the kitchen. I'm trying out a new recipe and I could use your input."

"For what?"

"**Lavender** creme brulee."

"Lavender?"

A Missing Mom and Mutt Munchies

"Mmhm. It's going to be delicious." She bounced out of her chair as a customer walked in.

I winced but fortunately she didn't see it since she was already headed back to the kitchen.

Lavender creme brulee? Why lavender? I know a lot of people like the scent and maybe the taste is nice, too, but ugh. There were so many other choices if you were going to make creme brulee. I'd had an amazing mango one once. But lavender? What ever happened to vanilla? Or chocolate? Or even coconut?

Ah well. It was Jamie. I knew no matter how odd it sounded to me she'd make it taste delicious. And at least she still needed my help with something...

CHAPTER 7

It turns out that a well-made lavender creme brulee is incredibly delicious. It has this delicacy to it that's absolutely heavenly. The iterations before that final sample were less so, but it was all worth it for the final product which Maggie, Greta, and I enjoyed while catching up that afternoon.

Hans, Greta's Irish Wolfhound, rested at her feet, as stalwart as ever, but I noticed that she slipped him a few treats here or there, something she'd never done before. And that she reached down to pet him frequently. He was also lying close enough to her to keep in touch with her foot at all times.

They'd been through a rough situation. I couldn't blame them for

A Missing Mom and Mutt Munchies

wanting the comfort of their closest companion. I'd had a hard enough time dealing with it and it wasn't even my dog that was hurt.

Greta was doing well, too. She looked as polished as ever in a bright purple silk top and trim black slacks, her white blonde hair pulled back in a simple chignon at the base of her neck. She was insanely wealthy, but she kept the jewelry to amazing but subtle pieces. I figured she was only a couple years older than me, but it was hard to tell. She could have just had very good work done.

We talked about Jamie and Mason's wedding options for a bit—a topic that fascinated Jamie and Greta far more than it did me. Who cared what flowers were in season? Or what the latest trend in bridal colors was? Or if there had to be a vegan food option just in case?

And did it really matter if there was a chocolate fountain and a photo booth? Would people care any less if they weren't adequately entertained?

It wasn't that I begrudged my friend a public celebration of finding the love of her life, or even the fact that she'd found someone. It was just that, well...

I hate weddings.

For some reason I'm always getting invited to weddings by close friends who seem to have all these other friends that I've never met. And I never have a plus one to bring, which means I generally get put at the "extras" table with a bunch of folks I've never met before who also don't have a significant other to bring and were probably only invited for arcane social reasons.

Basically, I fall into the same category as the second cousin twice removed who Aunt Betty insisted had to come but no one in the family even knows, and who was only invited because they figured she wouldn't come but then she did.

It's not that my friends don't want me there. They do. And it's not that I don't want to be part of the wonderful joining of their lives. I do. It's just that they're stressed and busy and not available the whole time and I get stuck making conversation with the weirdo next to

A Missing Mom and Mutt Munchies

me who's into something like bug collecting.

And there is never, ever a good-looking, intelligent, funny, interesting single man at one of those things. You'd think there would be, but no. At least not all four qualities in one. (Usually I can't even find a guy who has two of those qualities at a wedding, and if he does have two of them, single isn't one of the two.)

I was prepared to suffer through for Jamie, but that didn't mean I wanted to spend the next few months of my life hearing all the little details that led up to it.

So I was zoned out and brooding about the stupid article and how Matt was going to react when he read it when Greta turned to me. "How is your cop?"

"He's not my cop. He's just...a friend. And he seems to be fine. I mean, I don't know. I don't keep track of him. I'm not his keeper. But last time I saw him he seemed fine." I knew I sounded a little defensive, but he wasn't my cop. Not really.

Greta raised one slender eyebrow as she took a delicate bite of her creme brulee. "So you are still single then? I could bring my friend, Eduard, by to meet you?"

"No."

"You are not single?"

"I am not interested."

Greta had an unfortunate belief that a woman's first husband should be very old and very rich. Since she was probably in the double digits husband-wise and already obscenely rich herself that meant pushing men who met her criteria in my direction instead.

"I have better things to do with my time, Greta. Like figure out how to make the barkery actually thrive."

"Money would help with this, no? Eduard would help with this. He is a very generous man. And very smart. Very good at business."

"Greta..."

I was on the verge of saying something extremely impolite when I saw Sam, the red-headed freckled kid from the baseball game, ride his bicycle into the parking lot. His

A Missing Mom and Mutt Munchies

cheeks were decidedly pink under his baseball cap and there were spots of sweat on his t-shirt.

I pushed outside. "Sam, right? What are you doing here? Did you ride all the way from Creek? How long did that take you?" It took me twenty minutes by van, it had to have taken him a couple of hours on his battered red bike.

He tried to gather his breath to answer me, but I could see that he'd been crying so I immediately shuffled him inside. "Let me get you something to eat and a drink. You like Coke?"

He nodded. "Yes, ma'am, Mrs. Carver. Thank you."

I pointed him to a table near Greta and Jamie as I ran to the kitchen for a Coke and a chocolate croissant. I figured he probably wouldn't appreciate the buttery delicacy of what Jamie had accomplished, but chocolate and fat are always good choices for anyone remotely human, especially kids.

When I came back he was seated with Greta and Jamie. I was about to shoo him back to the table I'd pointed out to him, but Greta put her hand on his back and shook her head.

Instead I dragged a chair over to join them and set the Coke and croissant in front of him. "Sam, what are you doing here?"

He didn't answer right away. He was too busy drinking down half the Coke and tearing into the croissant. When he finally looked at me he had a smear of chocolate on the corner of his mouth. He'd somehow managed to get chocolate on his fingers, too.

"I need your help, Mrs. Carver."

"It's Miss Carver, not Mrs., but you can just call me Maggie. What's wrong?" I tensed as I remembered that ugly scene from the game the day before.

"My mom's missing. I saw that article in the paper about how you solve crimes." He reached for his backpack and pulled out a baseball-shaped piggy bank that jangled with change as he hefted it onto the table. "I want to hire you to find her."

A Missing Mom and Mutt Munchies

I opened my mouth to tell him no, but how could I? He was staring at me with those big brown eyes of his like a lost puppy.

"Sam…Ummm. I think you got the wrong idea from that article. But Matt, Mr. Barnes, your coach, I'm sure he can help you. He's a cop. It's his job to find people who go missing."

He hunched his shoulders and looked at the floor. "I called the cops. They won't listen to me. Said to leave it to the adults. But Vick won't do anything. He doesn't care. Said it's just like her to run off. Not the first time she's done it either. She'll come back eventually."

"Is Vick the guy from the game yesterday? The one who yelled at you?"

He nodded, but still wouldn't look at me. I was pretty sure he'd started crying again.

"And the woman? Was that your mom? The one who pulled him away when he got mad?"

He nodded again.

Aleksa Baxter

I flicked a glance at Jamie and Greta. "And she's gone?"

"Yeah. She wasn't there when I got home last night. And she wasn't there this morning either. Sometimes she's gone at night, but not in the mornings usually."

"Well, maybe she just needed to get away for a few hours. Vick seemed pretty mad yesterday. I know I wouldn't want to be around a man who was angry like that."

He hunched further into himself. "He's always angry. She doesn't seem to mind."

"But she has gone away before?"

He kicked the table. "You're just like them. You're just like the cops. It's my birthday tomorrow. We were supposed to go shopping today. She's never been gone for my birthday. Never. Something happened to her."

I pressed my lips together. I was way out of my depth on this one. The kid didn't need me. He needed the cops.

I mean, it was pretty obvious to me what must've happened. Only question was whether Sam's mom

A Missing Mom and Mutt Munchies

had run off to get away from her abusive boyfriend for a while or whether the ugly fight I'd seen coming when they walked away from the game had turned into something permanent.

Either way, I was not the person to handle it.

"Tell you what. I'll call Matt for you. And he'll look into it. I promise."

When Sam looked up at me I swear his eyes had doubled in size until he was like one of those cartoon characters that are all just sad eyes and floppy ears. "I want **you** to help, Miss Carver. Not him. I'll pay you." He pushed the piggy bank at me. "There's twenty-two dollars and thirty-one cents in there. It's all I have. Please. You have to help me."

My heart almost broke for the poor kid. "Sam…"

"Please." His eyes filled with tears. "I know she wouldn't leave me. I know it. She's hurt. You have to find her."

I sighed. "Okay. Fine. I'll help."

What else could I say? I would've happily and callously stepped over the body of a dead person to avoid getting sucked into another police investigation, but how do you turn your back on a sad little boy who just wants to find his mother?

"Thank you, Miss Carver." He flung himself out of the chair and hugged me.

I winced, wondering what kind of mess I'd gotten myself into now.

CHAPTER 8

The first thing I did, of course, was call Matt. Sam might not want the cops involved, but I did. And I was still hopeful that there was a chance I could pawn the whole thing off on someone more qualified.

"Maggie May. To what do I owe the pleasure?" Matt practically purred when he answered the phone.

I stepped out back with Fancy so Sam wouldn't hear me. As Fancy ran around sniffing everything and doing her business, I filled Matt in on what had happened.

I loved that space back there with its view of the mountains in the distance and the stream running by at the edge of the grassy area. Only Jamie and I ever used it, since it was fenced off on both sides, so it was like a little private oasis. A perfect spot to sit with a beer at the end of the day.

When Fancy was done with the basics, she gave me a quick look and then ran for the stream, settling herself into the middle of it with a happy little look as I glared at her. I swear, that girl knows how to take advantage of a situation, and she knew I wasn't going to yell at her or try to wade in and bring her back out when I was on the phone.

She is one smart little Newfie. (Smarter than me, I'm pretty sure.)

When I finished telling Matt about Sam's mom I asked, "Do you think Sam's right? That the cops aren't going to look into it?"

"I do. She's an adult. And she hasn't even been gone a day. Plus, from what I hear this isn't the first time Trish has pulled a runner. She's taken off at least once that I know of."

I paced back and forth. That was not what I'd wanted to hear. "Did Sam call about that one, too?"

A Missing Mom and Mutt Munchies

"No. I don't think anyone did. I heard about it when I was hanging out at the Creek Inn. It seems a couple months ago Trish walked in, a fresh shiner on her eye, looked around the place, zeroed in on some out-of-towner having a beer with his buddies, and within half an hour had the man convinced to take her to Wyoming with him when he left town the next day. Didn't come back for a week."

That wasn't a good sign. How do you tell a kid his mom won't be there for his birthday because she's a bit of a tramp that runs off with strange men?

I pinched the bridge of my nose, thinking.

Maybe this time was different. "Sam said his birthday's tomorrow. And that his mother has never been gone on his birthday before. Maybe this time it's worth investigating."

There was a long silence.

I waited Matt out as I watched Fancy come out of the stream and shake herself off and then go lie down in the shade along the fence.

Aleksa Baxter

She was going to be a muddy mess. Good thing she seemed to miraculously clean up from even the worst messes after a few hours. If not, my grandpa was going to have something to say about it.

I could almost picture Matt trying to figure out how to get me to drop the whole thing. But that wasn't going to happen, so I finally said, "I've gotta at least try to find her, Matt."

"No, you need to stay out of it. She probably got in a fight with Vick, took off, met someone else, went home with him and spent the day sleeping it off. She'll be back for the kid's birthday tomorrow. Just let it go."

"Sam rode his bike here all the way from Creek. That had to take hours. And you should've seen him, Matt. He probably cried most of the way here. I can't just let it go. He's a little boy who wants his mom there on his birthday. Doesn't he deserve that?"

"Maggie."

"Please help me. At least go by Vick's with me."

Matt sighed.

A Missing Mom and Mutt Munchies

"Please?" I don't like to beg, but in this case I was willing to make an exception.

There was a long silence on the other end of the line, so I continued, "You're taking some time off, right? Isn't this a better way to spend your time than fishing or watching Jack to see what trouble he'll get into? It's Sam's birthday tomorrow, Matt. He said she's never been gone on his birthday before. And you saw the way that man was with her at the game. I think he did something to her. What if she's injured and we could save her?"

"You need to stay out of their business, Maggie. It could be dangerous."

I didn't say anything. Of course it was going to be dangerous. The man had probably killed his girlfriend. But didn't Sam deserve to know what had happened to his mom?

"Maggie..."

I shook my head even though I knew Matt couldn't see it. Why did he have to be so darned stubborn?

"Don't you know me by now? I'm not going to stay out of it, Matt. You can come along and help me ask the questions that need to be asked, so we can find this little kid his mother. Or you can sit at home with Jack and worry about what's going to happen to me when I show up at Vick's door accusing him of murder. Your call."

"That's not fair."

"It may not be fair, but those are your choices."

Fancy watched me from where she'd laid down in the shade, one eyebrow raised. Even she knew I was playing dirty, but I didn't really care. This was about a little kid and his mom. I'd play as dirty as it took.

And I really needed Matt to say yes. If he didn't I was going to have to ask my grandpa for help, which I did not want to do.

As impetuous as I might be, even I knew that it wouldn't be smart to confront Vick alone.

"Damn it, Maggie. Why can't you just leave things be?" Matt growled.

A Missing Mom and Mutt Munchies

I knew when he cussed that I had him. "So you'll meet me at my place in an hour?"

"Yeah. See you there."

"Thank you," I practically sang into the phone. I should've probably toned it down a bit given Matt's reluctance to get involved, but I was so happy I wouldn't have to rope my grandpa into helping out that I couldn't help it.

CHAPTER 9

I sincerely apologized to Jamie for leaving her—yet again—to take care of things at the barkery. It's a good thing she's such a go-with-the-flow even-keeled sort of person or I was pretty sure I'd have lost her as a friend by that point.

She just smiled and said, "We should've put some money on your statement that you wouldn't get involved in another police matter."

"Well, **technically**, it's not a police matter since they wouldn't look into it. But I am sorry to do this again."

She laughed. "Don't worry about it, Maggie. I completely understand. He rode all the way here. His mom is missing. You have to help. If you didn't, I would. Now go. I've got this."

A Missing Mom and Mutt Munchies

"You're sure?"

"Positive."

"Thank you." I gave her a quick hug before shuffling Fancy and Sam out to my van.

Jamie is one of the best people I know. And competent as all get out. She could run the café, the barkery, and the world without breaking a sweat if she wanted to, so at least I knew the place was in good hands and I could focus on Sam and his mom.

During the twenty-minute drive home Sam talked non-stop. I heard about what he and his mother had done on every single birthday since he'd turned five, the names of all of his friends at school, the names of the three older boys who bullied him at lunch each day, what those boys had done to him over the last school year, his plans for when he was grown up and could fight back, as well as the fact that he planned on being a superhero, a cop, an astronaut, and a fighter pilot. Oh, and a billionaire. And...

It was a lot.

Aleksa Baxter

By the time I walked in the front door at home I was ready for a nap or a Tylenol or maybe both, but that wasn't going to happen. Because sitting together at the kitchen table, their faces grim, were my grandpa and Matt.

I should've known Matt wouldn't keep my grandpa out of it, but I gave him a really nasty glare anyway.

I grabbed ice cream from the freezer for Sam, Fancy, and myself (puppy ice cream for Fancy) and in an artificially cheery voice said, "Hey, Sam, why don't you go out back with Fancy. I need to talk to these guys for a minute."

Once they were outside I turned to deal with the dual threat of my grandpa and Matt. I figured I needed every advantage I could get, so rather than sit at the table I leaned against the fridge as I carefully unwrapped my ice cream bar. (Technically a salted caramel gelato bar—yum—but whatever.)

"Maggie May." My grandpa folded his hands on the table, giving me flash backs to being grounded when I was a kid.

A Missing Mom and Mutt Munchies

"Don't even try to talk me out of this, Grandpa. I am not letting that little boy spend his birthday wondering where his mom is if I can do something about it."

My grandpa tapped his fingers together as he glared me down. "Vick Kline is the worst sort of scum. You think he won't hurt you if he did this? He will. You even suggest he did it, he'll hurt you. Just for fun."

I barely stopped myself from rolling my eyes. "It's not like I'm going alone. Matt's coming with me. And this Vick guy can't be stupid enough to go after a cop."

My grandpa raised one eyebrow as if questioning that assessment. "Matt isn't going with you."

I stared at Matt, hurt. "You're not? But you said you would."

"I'm a police officer, Maggie." He rubbed the back of his neck with a wince. "And after that little newspaper article today my boss told me very specifically to keep you out of any and all police investigations."

71

"But it's not a police investigation. If it was, I wouldn't need to do this. Why don't you tell him that?"

He laughed. "Because I don't really want to push back on him right now. That would not be good."

"Look, all I'm asking is that you come along while I ask a guy a few questions. That's all."

He shook his head. "I can't do it, Maggie. Especially if you're planning on accusing him of murder. How am I going to explain that if he goes and complains?"

"I don't know. You're smart. You can think up something."

"I can't do it, Maggie."

I looked back and forth between them. "So you guys just want me to drop it? Well, that's not going to happen."

My grandpa reached for his non-existent cigarettes and then glared at his coffee like he wished it were whiskey instead. "We know. That's why I'm coming with you."

"Grandpa...I don't think that's a good idea."

A Missing Mom and Mutt Munchies

(I know. If Matt had turned me down originally I'd planned on turning to my grandpa, but the more I thought about getting him involved with confronting a potentially dangerous man, the more that seemed like a really volatile combination that could end up with my grandpa in jail. Or worse.)

"Maggie May, don't you even start with me. I may be old, but I survived years in prison surrounded by men like Vick Kline. I know how to handle a man like that."

"That's what I'm worried about."

He snorted.

"Promise me before we go that you aren't going to do anything that would require someone to call the cops."

He very deliberately took a sip of his coffee instead of answering.

Great. So now my choices were go on my own—which was not a good idea and we all knew it—or take my grandpa who was likely to do something I'd regret witnessing and that might make me an accessory to something I didn't want to be an accessory to.

Or I could just let it go. Walk away because it wasn't my business if some woman who ran off on a regular basis happened to do so the day before her kid's birthday.

Even if her kid had ridden his bike all that way to find me and ask for my help.

But that wasn't me. Jamie was right. If I could help Sam, I was going to do it.

Just then Fancy ran inside followed by Sam who was screaming and trying to slap at her. I was about to tell him that no one, and I mean no one, yells at my dog. And certainly no one hits my dog unless they want me to hit them. But then I saw the two little paws sticking out of the side of Fancy's mouth.

She'd caught a bunny.

As if things weren't bad enough.

"Fancy, drop it. Right now," I said, my voice whipping out at her.

She did.

A Missing Mom and Mutt Munchies

But then it moved. So she picked it back up.

The look she gave me said, "I dropped it like you asked me to, so don't glare at me like that." (I swear, sometimes she is too clever by half. It's like having a mischievous twelve-year-old boy around all the time.)

"Drop it," I snapped again.

She did.

"Leave it," I said before she could pick it back up. I stepped forward. "Go. Outside. Now."

Fancy cried at me, but she went outside, tail tucked down and head bowed. She knew she was in trouble, she just didn't know why.

"You too, Sam. Go back outside."

He looked at the slobber-covered bunny at my feet, but then followed her outside without argument.

I glanced down at the bunny, part of me hoping that it was already gone so I wouldn't have to figure out what you do with a baby bunny that your dog has scared half to death but hasn't killed.

Unfortunately, it was still breathing.

Or fortunately. I mean, I was glad it was alive and that Fancy hadn't killed it. But now I had one more thing to deal with. And I couldn't just put the thing back out in the yard. It was making no effort to go anywhere, just lying there on its side breathing fast. If I put it in the yard and it didn't recover it would certainly be dead.

But what else was I supposed to do with it? I was pretty sure there weren't a bunch of bunny rehabs out there. And I certainly didn't know the first thing about raising a bunny.

Plus, I didn't want a pet bunny. I just wanted my dog to have not killed the wild bunnies living in our yard.

I shook my head. "Someone get me a box."

I grabbed a dish towel from the drawer and turned back but neither Matt nor my grandpa had moved.

"Did you hear me? Someone get me a box."

Matt looked at the bunny and back at me. "Maggie, what are you going to do with a box?"

A Missing Mom and Mutt Munchies

"Put the bunny in it. Give it a safe place to recover. When it's better I'll put it back outside."

He and my grandpa exchanged a look.

"What?"

Matt looked like he wanted to say something, but instead he stood up. "You have a good box for rehabbing a bunny?" he asked my grandpa.

My grandpa nodded towards the hallway. "Should be something on the top shelf in the front closet."

When Matt came back he took the dish towel from me. "I'll take care of this. Why don't you and your grandpa go deal with Vick Kline before it gets dark. He should be home from work by now. He works the early shift at the mine."

"Are you sure?"

He nodded. "Yeah. Go."

I left, glad I wasn't actually going to have to deal with the bunny.

(I kinda knew there was probably nothing to be done for the poor bunny and that Matt was sparing me having to see that, but I pretended

Aleksa Baxter

that he really was going to create a little home for it in that box and that in a few hours it would be back under my grandpa's porch hopping around with all its little bunny friends. The alternative was just too sad to contemplate.)

CHAPTER 10

Vick Kline lived in one of a cluster of rundown trailer homes a few blocks from the ball park. There were no yards to speak of—the trailers were clustered too close together on a single lot. And no road either, just a dirt track that ran between them.

We parked on the street and walked towards the cluster of trailers, my grandpa leading the way. Clearly, he knew where he was going. I certainly didn't.

A woman in a big muumuu with bright flowers on it watched us with narrowed eyes. She was smoking a cigarette, her other hand wrapped around some sort of alcoholic beverage that probably consisted of cheap whiskey and generic soda on the rocks. A couple of kids a little older than Sam played in the dirt in front of her trailer and I wondered if one or both of them were the bullies Sam had told me about.

She nodded to my grandpa. "Lou. What brings you around?"

"Nat. Here to see Vick. Sam said Trish is missing. You seen her today?"

"No, but good to know where that kid got to. I was supposed to be watching him but he lit out of here on his bike a few hours ago." She took a long drag on her cigarette as she eyed me up and down.

I opened my mouth to ask if she'd bothered to be worried about him at all, but my grandpa grabbed me by the wrist and squeezed. He knew me too well.

"By the way, Nat, this is my granddaughter, Maggie May. Maggie May, this is Nat."

She nodded. "Seen you around. You have that dog thing in Bakerstown with the Green girl, right?"

"The Baker Valley Barkery and Café. Yes."

"Right. The dog thing." She narrowed her eyes as she blew out a

A Missing Mom and Mutt Munchies

stream of smoke. "People actually pay for that stuff?" (The word she used was not in fact "stuff" but it started with the same letter.)

"Some people do." I tried not to sound offended, even though I was. I failed.

"Huh. Who would've thought it."

My grandpa dragged me away before I could say anything else, calling out, "Thanks, Nat. Give my best to Don."

Nat nodded and went back to watching the kids who were jumping around and kicking at each other, shouting back and forth as they tried to re-enact some movie they'd seen somewhere. I heard a smack as one of the kids connected a little too hard and turned back to see Nat take another drag on her cigarette, completely unconcerned as the two kids rolled on the ground pummeling at one another.

My grandpa led the way to a faded green trailer at the end of the line. There were some rusted spots, but overall it looked well-tended for what it was. The curtains in the window were crisp and white with little edges of dark green lace.

He stepped up the wooden stairs and thumped on the door with his fist three times.

Vick answered the door in a white tank top and what looked like the same jeans from the day before. He scratched at his belly and I was treated to the sight of way too much hair in places I didn't want to know it existed. "What?"

"We're looking for Trish. She here?"

"No." Vick looked like he'd just woken up from a nap, the creases from the couch still visible on his face and what remained of his hair sticking up in at least three places.

"Where is she then?"

"How'm I supposed to know? I'm not her keeper."

I wanted to make some smart aleck comment about Sam and whether he'd even noticed the kid was gone, but my grandpa glared at me before he stepped into the trailer, forcing Vick to step back to avoid touching him.

A Missing Mom and Mutt Munchies

My grandpa filled the doorframe as he looked around the living area. "It's Sam's birthday tomorrow. He says they were supposed to go shopping today. Make sense to you that she's not here for that?"

Vick ran a hand through his greasy, receding hairline, smoothing it down. "No. She loves that kid more than anything."

"Then where is she?"

"I don't know. Look. Trish took off yesterday. We had a thing. Said some words. And then she tore out of here. I figured she'd be back last night. When she wasn't, I figured she'd be back today. She does that sort of thing."

"But she's not."

Vick met my grandpa's gaze for a brief moment and hunched his shoulders. "She does that sort of thing, too. Always looking to trade up. But she comes back eventually. I'm good to her. Better than most of the losers she finds for herself."

I stepped up to the base of the stairs. "Mind if we look around?"

83

Both he and my grandpa glared at me, but I glared right back. "What? You're going to take his word for it that she just took off like that? Do you know what she's done for each of Sam's birthdays? Treasure hunts and special picnics at the park. That sort of thing. And now we're just supposed to believe him that she didn't care this year because they got in a fight?"

Vick's eyes were black with hatred as he glared down at me.

My grandpa very deliberately braced his arm across the doorway between us. "She could be a little more polite about it, but she has a point, Vick. Show me around."

I stepped forward to join them, but my grandpa shook his head. "You stay out here. I'll be back in a minute."

I wanted to argue, but I knew I'd lose. Instead I walked around the perimeter of the trailer looking for any signs of foul play.

(And, no, I really had no idea what that would be. Pretty sure most killers don't intentionally leave a big

A Missing Mom and Mutt Munchies

pool of blood visible for anyone to see.)

There was nothing that looked the least bit suspicious.

No broken furniture. No rolled up rugs. No bloody baseball bats. Just a bunch of weeds and some rusted out car parts around back. The little bit I could see of each of the windows looked well-tended and clean, though. Seems wherever she'd disappeared to Trish had taken some pride in her home.

My grandpa didn't find anything either. He just shook his head as he stepped back outside.

He turned and shook Vick's hand. "Thanks, Vick. You'll let me know if she comes back?"

Vick nodded. "And if you find her you'll let me know?" He actually sounded concerned.

My grandpa nodded. "I will."

As we walked back to my grandpa's truck, I muttered, "You didn't have to be so friendly to him, you know. Even if he isn't the reason she's missing, he probably still beats her. And he's most definitely a drunk. I mean, look

85

at that woman who was supposed to be watching Sam today. A cigarette in one hand, a drink in the other..."

My grandpa grabbed my arm and pulled me to a stop. "Maggie May. Not everyone has a charmed life like you did."

I opened my mouth to protest that my life had been far from charmed, thank you very much, but the look he gave me made me snap it shut again.

"I know. You're life wasn't perfect." He leaned closer. "But you ever been hit?"

I shook my head. "No. Of course not."

"You ever had a parent gone for months or years because they were in jail?"

"No."

"You ever had to add water to your ketchup to make it last longer?"

"No." My dad had before my grandpa came into his life, I knew that, but I never had.

"Or sleep on a friend of a friend of a friend's couch because that was the

A Missing Mom and Mutt Munchies

only way to have a roof over your head that night?"

"No." I muttered the answer, wanting him to stop already. I got it. Other people were worse off.

"Then don't judge, Maggie." He gestured at the trailers. "You look at these people and you see what they aren't. So what if they don't have pretty yards in front of their homes. Or they drink and smoke a little more than you think is right. Or maybe they get so worn out and run down by life they lose it every once in a while. That doesn't make them bad people, Maggie May. It just means they're living in bad circumstances."

"Fine. Okay. But...If he was hitting her, that isn't right. And if he ever hit Sam..."

"Agreed. But I walked through that place and it was clean as a button. And that kid had three times as many clothes as either of them. I'm not saying Vick isn't a violent man or that he couldn't stand to lay off on the drink. But I don't think he did this. Wherever Trish is, it isn't because Vick put her there."

I pressed my lips together. I wasn't so sure. I mean, come on. Drunk man threatens woman and kid in public and then woman goes missing, how can you not think the drunk man is responsible?

But there was no point in arguing with my grandpa about it. Not after I'd just insulted his friend. "Okay. So if she did leave on her own, then where'd she go?"

"That's the question isn't it? Let's go home. Vick gave me a list of numbers you can call."

CHAPTER 11

We headed back home to regroup. I was surprised to find Jack there when we arrived. Especially since he was seated at the dining room table working a puzzle of a mountain meadow with Sam.

He glanced up when we walked through the door. "Hope you don't mind. We dug this out of the closet. Thought it would be more interesting than watching that big mutt wait to catch another bunny."

"Where's Matt?" I asked.

Jack glanced at Sam but the kid was focused on putting together a section of the puzzle border, his tongue sticking out of the corner of his mouth.

"He went to take that bunny to a friend of his who specializes in that sort of thing. Asked me to keep an eye on Sam while he was gone."

For a moment I got my hopes up about the fate of the poor little bunny Fancy had gotten ahold of. But when I caught my grandpa's smug look I realized Matt had taken it elsewhere to spare Sam knowing what had happened to it.

My grandpa leaned close and whispered, "**Now** are you going to let me take care of the rabbits?"

"No," I whispered back. "Because you'd take care of all of them. Fancy isn't fast enough to get more than one or two."

He shook his head and walked towards the kitchen. "You hungry, Jack? Want to stick around for dinner?"

"Sure. Why not?"

I was fine with having Matt over for dinner on a regular basis, but Jack was another story. Then again, he did seem to be doing well with Sam. At least the kid wasn't crying anymore. And since we'd found absolutely no sign of his mother, he needed someone to look after him.

A Missing Mom and Mutt Munchies

I followed my grandpa into the kitchen. "What are we going to do with Sam?"

"He can stay here or go with Jack until his mom's back."

"Vick didn't care about that?"

He shook his head. "Naw, he just wants Trish. If Sam comes along for the ride, fine. But when she's not there...He could care less what happens to that boy."

"Doesn't she have a mom or other relatives that can look after him?"

"Her mom is out of state. No other family. A few friends here or there. But usually when Trish disappears for a while Vick dumps Sam on Nat. The woman you met today."

"Oh."

He gave me a look that had me ducking my head in apology. "You have that list of numbers for me to call?"

He reached into the breast pocket of his flannel shirt and handed it over. I turned it around, trying to figure out which direction was up.

"What?"

"I'm just wondering if I'll be able to decipher your handwriting. Is that a two or a seven?"

"A two. Now get out of the kitchen and make those calls while I put something together for dinner."

As I grabbed my phone, my grandpa pulled a box of macaroni and cheese from the cupboard and rooted out some hot dogs from the fridge. I paused and stared at him. "You are not seriously going to fix mac n cheese with hotdogs for dinner are you?"

He nodded. "Yes, I am. It's the perfect dinner choice for kids."

Maybe in the seventies it was.

"There's not even a vegetable in that."

"Vegetables are over-rated. But you want a vegetable there's some canned peas in the cupboard."

He knew how much I hated canned peas. I'd once spent three hours sitting at the dinner table because I refused to eat those mushy, gushy nasty things and my grandma wouldn't let me leave until I'd cleaned my plate. I'm not really sure

A Missing Mom and Mutt Munchies

who won that battle of wills since I swallowed each one whole rather than eat it and she had to sit there the whole three hours to make sure I didn't ditch them down the drain when she wasn't looking.

I glared at him for a long moment, but my grandpa was in a mood, and when my grandpa was in a mood there was no point arguing with him because he could dig in harder than a diamond.

We'd all survive one night of bad food.

But hotdogs? This was one of those times when I wished I lived somewhere that had a Pizza Hut right around the corner. Unfortunately, delivery of any kind of food was non-existent in our little town or the neighboring towns for that matter. It was eat what you have on hand or drive to the next town over for a meal.

And since I didn't want to do that…

I took my phone out to the back porch so I could make my calls and check on Fancy at the same time. She'd stationed herself on the porch,

93

her nose poked through the slats, chin resting on the bottom rail as she watched the yard, completely motionless.

There was nothing to see, but that didn't seem to bother her. Clearly she'd found a spot she thought gave her a good vantage point for if or when another bunny showed up.

I walked to the other end of the porch and leaned on the side rail to dial the first number, the one for Trish's mom.

As the phone rang I glanced down to see two baby bunnies and two adult bunnies gathered together in the shade happily munching on the grass, having what looked to be a nice little family picnic.

I snorted. Of course that's how it would be. Fancy was so intent on looking for bunnies in one direction she'd completely missed the family gathering happening in the other direction.

No one answered at Trish's mom's house. The answering machine kicked in—and it was definitely a machine that I'd bet probably ran on

A Missing Mom and Mutt Munchies

tapes and everything—and informed me that she was sailing the seas in Mexico and wouldn't be back for a week.

I winced, but hung up without leaving a message. No point in worrying her when Trish would probably be back before she was. But hadn't anyone ever told her not to announce to the world that she'd be out of town and to please stop by and steal her things while she was away? It was like the people who posted on Facebook about all of their travel plans.

"Hey, world, look, I'm in Europe right now having an amazing time. Yes, of course that means that my house is unprotected because I even complained on here about having to board my dogs. Oh, and yes, that fancy schmancy TV I posted a picture of at Christmas is absolutely sitting in my front room right now."

Especially since most of the people who did that sort of thing also had seven hundred and fifty "friends" on Facebook. I'm sorry, but no. Those people are not all your friends. And if they are your friends, well, you probably aren't a very good friend to them.

(Sorry for my rant. I'm the small, close circle of friends type of person and take it personally when I run up against the "everyone is my friend" type who is more performing for an audience than forming friendships. But I digress. To each their own.)

After missing Trish's mother, I quickly worked my way down the rest of the list. There were two friends from high school who hadn't heard from her in days but agreed she'd never miss Sam's birthday, as well as an ex who hadn't heard from her either but did try to hit on me by inviting me to come over and check out his place if I wanted, because according to him I sounded like sunshine on the phone.

Seriously? Did that line ever work for him? It's about as bad as "Is your father a thief? Did he steal the stars and put them in your eyes?" Although not near as unique as the guy who once stopped me on the street to tell he liked the shape of my

A Missing Mom and Mutt Munchies

upper arms. (That one was probably a cannibal or something weird. Not my legs? My arms? Okay. Whatever.)

I even tried Trish's work, but that just earned me a long rant from the boss who said the only reason he'd given her two days off when he was short staffed was because of Sam's birthday. He threatened to fire Trish if she'd pulled a runner rather than do what she'd said she was going to do which, according to him, was take Sam down to Denver for a day at the zoo.

After I hung up from that call I needed a long moment to recover my sunny disposition (ha), so I stared at the bunnies as they happily munched on the grass without caring at all that I was right there watching them. Fearless little things.

I didn't know what else to do about Trish. We'd tried her home and struck out there, I'd tried her friends, I'd tried her work, I'd even tried her worthless ex.

But then I remembered that Trish had pulled her last runner by picking up a random guy at a bar. I figured the dive bar in Bakerstown where

Marla worked was more her speed, but that the Creek Inn was closer and more likely to have the type of easy mark Trish could charm. She might have bad taste in men, but she was still an attractive woman so could pull a higher class of guy if needed.

I dialed Abe, the not openly gay but so gay owner of the Creek Inn, and also one of my favorite people in the entire county.

"Hello?"

"Hey, Abe, it's Maggie Carver. How are you?"

"Good, Maggie. When are you going to come in and visit us at the Inn? I'm starting to feel hurt that you haven't dropped by. Maybe I'll just have to make my next barkery order a delivery."

Abe was also one of my best customers. He and his partner Evan came by on a regular basis to pick up dog treats for their St. Bernard, Lucy Carrots.

I'd yet to make it to the Creek Inn to return the favor, though. Probably because I was in my pajamas curled up on the couch by six most nights.

A Missing Mom and Mutt Munchies

And bars are just…not my scene. Too much noise. Too many drunks. And men who try to grope you before they even talk to you…

Yeah, not a place I'd willingly go.

Not that Abe would run a place like that. But in a small town where the pickings were slim I figured a reasonably attractive woman walking into a bar was going to attract some attention no matter how nice the place. And after being as charming as I could manage at work all day I didn't have much left for random creeps. Even well-meaning ones.

"I will someday, I promise. Might even do so tonight, depending on what you have to say."

"Really? Do tell."

"Um, do you know Trish Mullens? Redhead with questionable taste in men?"

He laughed. "Yeah, she's in here fairly regular."

"Was she in there last night by any chance?"

He took a moment to think about it. "Yeah, I think she was. We have a group in right now and I remember her talking to one of them. Last night was the only night they've made it to the bar since they've been here."

"Any chance she left with one of them?"

"Can't say I noticed. Why?"

"She's missing. Didn't come home last night. And it's her son's birthday tomorrow so he's convinced something bad must've happened to her."

"I didn't know you and Trish Mullens were friends."

"We're not. But the cops won't look into it yet, so I said I would."

He harrumphed. "That article go to your head? You taking on clients now?"

"No. But that stupid article is why Sam Mullens rode his bike from Creek to the barkery and offered me all the money in his piggy bank to look for her. What was I supposed to do? The cops won't look for her yet because she's not considered missing for at least a day. And even if it had been a day they wouldn't be all that concerned because it seems she likes to take off on a regular basis."

A Missing Mom and Mutt Munchies

"That she does. She'll probably be back tomorrow."

"Yeah, probably. But I have to give it a try for the kid, you know. You think those guys will be back tonight?"

"Maybe. They're staying here and not much else to do unless they want to drive all the way to Masonville."

"You mind texting me as soon as they show up?"

"Sure. Happy to."

"Thanks."

I hung up and turned to look at Fancy, because she was still staring intently out at the yard while the bunny family picnic continued at my feet. "You are not a very good bunny dog, do you know that?"

She ignored me.

"Do you understand that there is a whole family of bunnies that has been having dinner over here while you're staring off into space over there?"

She still ignored me.

I pointed over the railing. "Bunny, Fancy. Bunny."

She turned to look at me.

"Bunny." I pointed again.

She slowly stood and looked in the direction I was pointing.

(Don't worry. I had no expectation that she'd catch any of them. She's slow. And most bunnies are fast. Turns out the only reason she'd caught that bunny earlier in the day was because it had frozen out in the middle of the yard and all she'd had to do was duck her head and pick it up from the grass.)

(Plus she was up on the porch and I figured they'd run as soon as she made a move towards them.)

I didn't want her to catch them, but I did figure they needed to be just a little bit more scared than they were. Maybe scared enough to stop hanging out in my grandpa's yard before he took matters into his own hands.

"Bunny, Fancy" I said, again, nodding my head towards the bunnies who'd finally deigned to notice my existence but still hadn't bothered to run away.

A Missing Mom and Mutt Munchies

Fancy finally came over to see what I was pointing at and saw the bunnies. She turned and ran for the ramp and then galumphed after them but they scattered and hid without even breaking a sweat.

At which point she started to cry very loudly and look at me like it was all my fault somehow. Shaking my head, I went back inside to have the kind of dinner I hadn't had since I was a kid. (And hadn't wanted to have since I was a kid either.)

"Enough, Fancy. Dinner."

CHAPTER 12

My grandpa was gone when I walked back inside, but the food was ready.

Turns out Lesley had called and asked him to come over. Bill had passed earlier that day and she wasn't doing so well being alone in their house all by herself. (She had kids and grandkids but they'd left her alone because she'd asked for the space. Plus, I think sometimes it takes talking to someone who's been through what you've been through at a time like that and my grandpa had, unfortunately, been there himself just a couple years before.)

It was good for Lesley that she had my grandpa to turn to, but I worried about him. As much as I liked Lesley—and I did, she was a good, kind woman—I wasn't entirely happy

A Missing Mom and Mutt Munchies

with the thought of my grandpa moving on.

I mean, he'd been married to my grandma for forty years. Is it even possible to move on from something like that? And what does it say if you can?

Those were my thoughts at the time. What can I say, I can be petty sometimes.

But I knew deep down that if someone moves on after losing a love like that it isn't because they didn't love deeply. It's because they were once loved so much that they crave that connection with another person and can't live without it.

Once I'd acknowledged that I also acknowledged that I should be grateful that my grandpa actually had the potential to find that type of connection again with Lesley. It's not often that people have a chance at that kind of love twice in their life.

Still, though.

My grandpa was all I had left. I didn't want to lose him and I didn't want to see him hurt.

🐾 🐾 🐾

Aleksa Baxter

We squeezed four chairs around the kitchen table because the dining room table was still covered by the half-finished puzzle. It was a little tight moving around in the kitchen with the table pulled away from the wall and Fancy sprawled next to my chair, but we made it work.

We couldn't talk about Sam's missing mom over dinner. At least not in the sort of "where do you think she ran off to" way I wanted.

At least Fancy did actually join us for dinner. She laid down next to me and daintily ate mac n cheese and hot dogs off her sharing plate I put on the floor. I had to tell Sam not to feed her, though, because he would've probably given her half his meal just for the fun of watching her eat each bite and then gaze up at him with her sad amber eyes begging for the next one.

She didn't make it through the whole meal, though. About halfway through I hiccupped. (It happens sometimes if you drink as much Coke as I do.) When I did that Fancy jerked her head up and stared at me

A Missing Mom and Mutt Munchies

with horror in her eyes, her entire body tensed to flee.

Hiccups being hiccups, I did it again, and she scrambled to her feet and ran outside, looking back at me like I was suddenly possessed.

Who knew a hundred and forty pound dog could be scared of someone with hiccups? But she was.

At least it made Sam laugh. He giggled his head off and wouldn't stop talking about it for the next five minutes.

After that Sam and Jack pretty much dominated the dinner conversation with a debate about the various superheroes and which was the best one.

I would've never expected it, but Jack got right down in there with the details, debating whether super strength was better than the ability to fly, and what x-ray vision could really be used for.

I caught Matt's eye at one point and raised my eyebrows as if to say, "Look at that? Who knew Jack would be so good with kids?"

He nodded and watched Jack with a thoughtful, but slightly sad look on his face.

After dinner I asked Jack to check Trish's Facebook account to see if she'd made any posts, but she hadn't. He also sent her a private message to let her know he had Sam with him, just in case.

I found it interesting that Jack had stayed Facebook friends with her even after they'd broken up and he'd left town. I tried to talk to him about it, but he shrugged me off. Whatever his reasons, there was more to it than "Never occurred to me to unfriend her."

I would've pushed more—just to annoy Jack more than for any other reason and because I'm always curious about those sorts of things—but Abe texted me to let me know the guys who'd been talking to Trish the night before were there.

I showed my phone to Matt. "I should go talk to these guys and I don't know if or when my grandpa's going to be back. You think you can go to a bar with me without getting

A Missing Mom and Mutt Munchies

in trouble? Otherwise I'll have to take Jack with me."

"No way are you and Jack going to a bar together."

"Is that so? And why not?"

Jack winked at me. "It's alright. Maggie and I'll get our alone time some other day. Sam and I can hold down the fort here until you get back."

Matt glared at him, but didn't say anything.

"Come on, Matt. Let's get going. No idea how long those guys are going to stay there."

As I grabbed my purse, Jack added, "You two don't do anything I wouldn't do."

I turned to look at him. "**Is** there anything you wouldn't do, Jack?"

"Good question." He swaggered towards me. "I figure you should never rule out any possibilities. Who knows what fun you'll miss?"

"Come on, Maggie, let's go." Matt frowned as he led me out the door, but I just laughed. Jack was trouble,

Aleksa Baxter

no doubt about it, but he was amusing, too.

CHAPTER 13

As we were walking towards Matt's truck—a blue Ford F-250 extended cab that I always had to hop to get into—my phone rang.

It was my old boss, Karen. When I'd quit I'd told her to call me if a question came up that she thought only I could answer. I didn't want to leave her in the lurch, and even though I'd tried to pass on as much as I could before I left, I knew there'd always be a few things that I could answer in a minute that would take hours or days for someone else to track down.

Even though I had no intention of ever going back to that job or that city I also didn't believe in burning bridges. So I answered as Matt held the door for me.

"Hey, Karen. What's up?"

"Hey, Maggie. How are you? How's the dog bakery going?"

(She wasn't the type to ever use the word barkery. It was too cutesy for her.)

"It's going well," I lied. No point in telling her I was feeling like a failure. "And how are you?"

We made some polite chit-chat for a few minutes as Matt drove through the winding canyon between Creek and the Creek Inn.

The whole time we were talking I was wondering what on earth was going on because Karen was not the type for small talk. I remember the first time I met her I asked if she knew someone who had worked at her old employer. As you do. Trying to form connection. She'd said "Yes," and then immediately changed the topic to something business-related.

I'd worked for her for five years and she'd been like that the whole time. Not an easy fit for someone as unfiltered as myself who actually likes to be friends with the people I work with.

A Missing Mom and Mutt Munchies

Which meant that her taking the time to chit chat the way she was before she got to the point did not bode well.

Finally, I couldn't stand the suspense anymore. "Look, Karen, I'm headed somewhere and going to have to get off the phone in a minute. Was there something specific you were calling about?"

She almost sounded relieved when she said, "Actually, yes. Remember the Devinson project?"

"Yeah."

It was one of the most challenging and annoying projects I'd ever worked on. I'd liked the challenge part of it, but the rest...Ugh. Probably part of the reason I'd finally hit my breaking point and decided to leave.

"They want to do a Phase II to build out what we proposed in Phase I."

"Congratulations. That's great. How many years of work is that going to be for you?" I put a subtle emphasis on the **you** part of that sentence.

"Three. But they had one condition."

Aleksa Baxter

My gut clenched. I did not like where this conversation was heading. "Oh?"

Matt pulled the truck into the gravel parking lot in front of the Creek Inn and killed the engine as Karen said, "They won't hire us to do the project unless you're involved."

"What? That's ridiculous. You don't need me." I gave Matt a quick sorry glance as he settled in to wait for my call to end.

"We tried to tell them that. But Craig is convinced that it just won't be the quality he wants it to be if you aren't involved."

(He was probably right. That didn't mean the project wouldn't be a success, though.)

I drummed my fingers on the dash. "Did you tell him I quit and moved to Colorado to start a barkery?"

"I did."

"And?"

"He told me to make you an offer you can't refuse. So here it is…"

Before I could stop her she'd laid out the details.

A Missing Mom and Mutt Munchies

It was good money. **Really** good money.

I'd earned enough before to comfortably live on my own in DC, which is not a cheap city to live in. This offer was three times that. **And** they'd include housing right by the client site. **And** they'd pay for day care for Fancy.

It was a dream offer.

If going back to what I'd been doing before was in any way what I wanted to do with my life.

I opened my mouth to tell her no, but she beat me to the punch on that one, too. "I don't want an answer right now, Maggie. Think about it. I'll call you back in a few days. Just remember, we don't get this project without you. So we're all counting on you. I'll email a copy of the contract for your review."

"Karen..."

"Just in case. Give it some serious thought, Maggie. Please. We need you on this." She hung up.

I stared at the phone for a long moment. It would've been easier if I could just tell her no instead of having to think about all that money. And how they needed me.

She knew just how to push my buttons.

I could probably turn down the money even if that made me a fool and I regretted it in five years when I was begging space on my friends' couches.

But to let down a team? To cost them a three-year project? That was going to be a lot harder to do.

It would've been one thing if I thought Jamie needed me, too, but with her comments about Paris it was pretty clear she was looking for a way out. Or at least, dreaming of something other than running a small town café with her best friend.

So I had Jamie who probably wanted out and didn't know how to say it, a barkery that wasn't living up to my expectations, and now a job offer that was almost too good to refuse where other people would suffer if I said no.

I shook my head when Matt opened his mouth to say something. "Later. Right now let's see if we can't find

A Missing Mom and Mutt Munchies

Trish and get this over with." I forced myself to sound cheerful even though a sick ball of stress had settled right in my gut.

CHAPTER 14

The Creek Inn was a valley staple. It had existed in one form or another since the first families showed up and built their first cabins. Abe and Evan hadn't owned it all that time, obviously. They'd only been around for the last five years or so. What on earth had possessed them to abandon their life in suburban Atlanta to run a small town bar and hotel in the mountains of Colorado, I do not know. But they seemed to like it. And being the owners of the Inn gave them an instant acceptance they probably wouldn't have found otherwise.

The Inn in its current incarnation was a tall white-washed building with green trim along the sloped roof and downspouts. Inside the bar portion it was one giant room with a long bar

A Missing Mom and Mutt Munchies

that stretched the length of the back wall, polished wooden tables scattered around the place, and a single dilapidated pool table (bar size, not regulation) and dart board tucked in the corner near the restrooms.

Everything was worn but clean. The walls were covered with Colorado paraphernalia of one sort or another, including a large selection of the old Colorado license plates (white lettering on green) that I would always think of as the real version. That new white with green lettering deal? Yeah, no. Those were not Colorado plates even if it had been twenty or so years since the changeover.

Abe waved at us as soon as we walked in. "What can I get you?"

In the interest of looking like Matt wasn't there helping me with what should be a police investigation, we each ordered a beer. They had Laughing Lab on tap so I went with that. It's a nice brown beer made by a brewery in Colorado Springs that I've always enjoyed.

Aleksa Baxter

Matt ordered a Coors Light. I was going to tease him about it, but before I could he pointed out that he was driving us back so he needed to keep the alcohol content as low as possible. That made enough sense that I didn't give him a hard time about the fact that his beer could likely be confused with yellow-tinged sparkling water.

We chatted with Abe and Evan for a few minutes as Abe poured our beers. They were headed to Canada for a week of heli-hiking on Monday which sounded like a ton of fun to me. Imagine being helicoptered to the top of some mountain peak it might take days to reach and then getting to hike around from there. I'd wanted to do something similar in New Zealand with a helicopter that dropped you at the top of a glacier, but the weather hadn't cooperated. Someday I'd get back there and make it happen.

Or I'd go to Canada where the weather was more predictable and heli-hike there instead. Right after I won the lottery. (Or completed a three-year project I didn't really want

A Missing Mom and Mutt Munchies

to do that would take me away from my family, friends, and Colorado...)

I reached for my purse to pay for my beer but Matt handed his card over before I could even get ahold of my wallet.

"Thanks. Next one's on me," I said, but he shook his head.

"You're not buying your drinks as long as I'm around. My mom would never forgive me for it."

I was tempted to launch into a lengthy discussion of how frickin' complicated it was to figure out when to pay for your beer or not when you're a woman. When I was younger men just bought my drinks, so I got used to that. But then I went to work out of college and most of the guys I worked with treated me like one of the guys and expected me to chip in, which I did. But it was my MBA program which really messed me up, because the guys would each buy a round and it was hard to get in there to pay for a round myself. But if I didn't manage to do so then the guys in my study group would give me a hard time for mooching off of everyone. Which I wasn't trying to do. But if someone puts a beer in your hand, what do you say?

You want me to pay, I'll pay. You don't, I won't. But what am I supposed to do? Hit people to be allowed to buy the next round?

I finally got to the point where all I wanted to do was run my own tab, buy my own drinks, and everyone who wanted to give me a hard time for making it all so confusing could just go jump in a lake somewhere.

Of course getting to that point then messed things up when it came to dating...

So...

Ugh.

Best to drink at home alone and not even deal with it.

To avoid going off on that rant on poor Matt who didn't deserve it, I took a long, long sip of my beer instead. Matt wanted to buy me beers? Good for him. One more mark in his favor.

As we leaned against the bar, Abe pointed to a group of four men sitting in the corner by themselves and told

A Missing Mom and Mutt Munchies

us those were the ones Trish had been talking to the night before.

They looked like yuppies with their nice shoes, khaki pants, collared shirts that had little brand emblems on the chest, and close-cut hair-dos that were trim but not military trim. (If such a thing as yuppies still exists. It does in my world. Basically they looked like a bunch of guys who probably wouldn't try to change a tire if they got a flat but would instead call an Uber to pick them up and AAA to fix it for them.)

"How should we do this?" Matt asked. "You want to take the lead, or you want me to?"

"How about you hang back and let me go chat with them."

Matt frowned at me. "A woman's missing. One of those guys could be responsible."

"Really? Look at them. You think one of those guys could take Trish? Please."

"If I'm going to hang out here at the bar while you do all the work why'd you have me come along at all?"

Aleksa Baxter

I gave him my best smile. "Because you're good company. Plus if they're not the citified types they look to be you can rescue me when I get in over my head." I batted my eyes at him.

He just took another sip of his beer but I could see the annoyance in his eyes. Probably figured that was exactly what was going to happen. But, seriously, this group was not going to be a problem. Not unless someone scratched their Mercedes.

I strolled over to them and they perked up when they caught sight of me. Couldn't blame them. It was a small town and they weren't anywhere near where single women were likely to hang out, so I was pretty much their only viable option if that's what they were looking for.

"Mind if I join y'all?" I asked.

(I don't know why, but it seems I turn Southern when I'm flirting with strangers. It's some weird thing I've never understood, but there you have it. It works in some odd way, though, so I've never bothered to fix it.)

A Missing Mom and Mutt Munchies

One of the guys looked me over while another pulled over a chair and the other two shuffled to the side to make room for me.

"So," I asked, "what brings y'all to town?"

Within a few minutes I had the whole story. It seemed they were a group of high school friends who liked to take a trip together each year even though they'd now scattered to various big cities along the east coast. One of the guys had just relocated to San Francisco for work so they'd moved that year's choice of location to Colorado to cut him a break. They'd been hiking that morning, rafting the day before, and fishing the day before that and were headed back home in the morning.

I teased them a bit about a boy's trip in a town that didn't offer a lot more than fishing and rafting. No night life. No ladies to flirt with.

Turned out three of the four were happily married so that was a big part of it. Best to avoid temptation as one of them put it.

"Lance has done alright for himself, though," one of the guys added, elbowing the guy who'd grabbed me a chair.

He blushed as he ran his hands through his dark hair. "Not really."

"What about that chick last night? The redhead. You were getting pretty friendly when I left."

I perked up. "Trish? She's a good friend of mine. Not a lot of redheads around these parts. You guys hook up?"

He scratched his chin. "Nah. It was definitely headed that way but then this guy walks in, throws an arm around her shoulder, and pulls her away. Said it had been a long time and they should catch up but she didn't look too happy about it and he didn't look too friendly."

I described Vick to him, but he shook his head. "No, that wasn't him. This guy was really tall and skinny with stringy blonde hair."

One of the other guys elbowed him in the ribs. "And you just let her go that easy, huh? No wonder you're still single."

A Missing Mom and Mutt Munchies

The first guy shuddered. "If you'd seen this guy, you would've let her go, too. One look and I knew I wanted nothing to do with him. Reminded me of **Deliverance**."

I stared him down for that one. I swear, one movie with crazy people living in the mountains and suddenly anyone who isn't the type to blend in a city reminds a guy of **Deliverance**.

"That's a bit extreme, don't you think?"

"Sorry, but he was scary." The guy crossed his arms and looked away. Clearly not the type to hurt a fly let alone a woman.

I looked around, but no one matched that description. "Hm. I wonder who it was. You catch a name?"

He shook his head.

"Did she seem scared at all?"

"No. Didn't seem happy about it, but didn't seem scared either. I waited around for another ten minutes or so, but she never came back in, so I called it a night. Like you said, not a lot of choice around here."

"Never came back in? So they went outside to talk?"

He nodded. "Yeah, they did."

One of the other guys interrupted, "Enough about your friend. She lost her chance. But here you are, and here Lance is, and one last night to..."

I laughed and shook my head. "Can't, sorry. I'm not the one night kind of girl. Plus, my ride wouldn't appreciate it much if I ditched out on him." I nodded towards Matt who was watching us very intently. "Speaking of. Better get back to him. Nice meeting you."

I made my way back to the bar certain that Lance was not the one responsible for Trish's disappearance. Which meant we needed to figure out who Mr. Stringy Hair was and what he'd done to Trish.

CHAPTER 15

I told Matt and Abe what I'd found out.

"You see anyone like that here last night?" I asked.

Abe shook his head. "No. But we were busy. I could've just missed it."

Matt looked at the table of guys one more time. "You're sure it couldn't be one of them? Maybe they just lied to you."

"I'm not usually that off about people."

He raised an eyebrow at me.

So I'd accused a few people I shouldn't have of murder and completely missed a few others that really were murderers. That didn't make me a bad judge of character.

Resisting the urge to stick my tongue out at him, I said, "You want to go talk to them yourself, feel free Mr. Super Cop."

He thought about it. He really did. But then he shrugged it off. "You're probably right." But that didn't keep him from watching them until they finally left.

I looked at Matt. "Well, what now? You have a database of skinny men with stringy blonde hair who might know Trish?"

"Not one I can access." He glanced at the pool table. "But since we're here, how about we play a game of pool or two?"

I bit my lip. Me and pool....

It was tempting. Very tempting. But Sam's mom was missing and I was no closer to finding her. What would I tell him if he found out I'd stopped to play pool instead of trying to find the guy who'd taken his mom?

Matt leaned closer. "Maybe that guy will come back in tonight. Don't want to leave too soon, do we?" He flashed me a wicked smile. "Plus, you know you want to beat me at something.

A Missing Mom and Mutt Munchies

Since you've failed with Scrabble, maybe you can make it up with pool."

Maybe...

I studied the table, moving into hustler mode. "What makes you think I can even play?"

"Way I heard it your dad was a pool shark back in the day."

I shook my head. "My grandpa talks too much. But, yeah, my dad could hold his own with a pool cue."

"I can't believe he wouldn't have taught his daughter to play, too."

I eyed the table. It had been years since I'd played, but some things you never lose, and I was pretty sure pool was one of them.

There'd been a time in my life when playing pool was my personal form of meditation. I'd go to the local pool hall, pay for an hourly table, and sink into the zone for a couple of hours as I tried to clear the table in as few shots as I could.

I loved pool. And it had been far too long. I rolled my shoulders. "Alright. Let's do this. But don't be surprised when you lose."

131

He'd probably beat me, but pool's a mental game as much as anything. And if I could put him off his game with trash talking, I was going to do it.

"Oh, I'm not going to lose. Trust me on that." He led the way to the table.

The cues were warped, of course. I don't think I've ever been to a bar that didn't have warped cues. I rolled the two choices we had across the table and instead of smoothly rolling along the felt one of them thumped its way across and the other veered sharply to the side.

I chose the one that veered over the one that thumped. Figured it was the less warped of the two.

"You can break," I told Matt as I chalked my cue getting pale blue chalk dust on my hand.

"You sure?" he asked.

"Unless you're good enough to clear a rack off the break?"

If he was that good, I was going to lose. And badly. Unless he was too pampered to manage on a bar table with a warped cue. I'd once played with a guy who could only make

A Missing Mom and Mutt Munchies

shots if he was using his own custom graphite cue that required him to wear a special glove. Nice enough guy, but really? That's not playing pool. That's...something else entirely.

As I watched Matt chalk his cue and line up the cue ball I could see he was more than just a casual player, but I still didn't want to break. I've never been particularly good at it and I figure it's always better to have the balls spread out than clustered together. Let's you focus more on the shot you want to take than on what to do about the mess that's still left.

It was a good break. He made two balls right away and at least three others reached the far end of the table. He sunk another two before it was my turn.

I'll give it to him. He had solid skills. And he knew how to set up his shots.

A lot of guys have no finesse when they play. It's all about hitting the ball as hard as they can and then hoping the ball lands somewhere good for the next shot. But Matt didn't play that way. He never used more force than was needed to get the ball in the pocket and the cue ball where he needed it for the next one.

Actually, other than his preference for bank shots he and I played a lot alike.

Me, I'm all about the cut shot. Geometry was not my favorite class, by far, but I can always see those angles no matter how unlikely they might be.

A few times early on I saw Matt raise an eyebrow in question when I went for a side pocket cut shot instead of the end of the table straight-in shot. But after I made the third or fourth one, he expected it.

The first game was a close one. It got down to just the eight ball.

But I won. Of course.

"Best of three?" Matt asked.

I nodded. "But I need another beer. Be right back."

"I got it." Matt got Abe's attention and signaled for two more beers.

We were close on the second game, too, but Matt won that one. He'd adjusted his leaves to account for my preference for cut shots which made

A Missing Mom and Mutt Munchies

him a really smart player, but didn't make me particularly happy.

That meant we had to play a third game, but I didn't mind. I was enjoying myself in a way I hadn't in a long time.

The third game went down to the eight ball, too.

As Matt leaned in to take his final shot, I leaned close (on the side where he wasn't holding the pool cue, thank you very much) and let my hair fall along his arm as I whispered in his ear. "Hm. You think you can make that? I mean it's not the easiest of shots, is it?"

What can I say? All's fair in love and pool.

He paused and looked at me, our faces inches apart. "Maggie. Stop trying to cheat."

"What are you talking about? I'm just saying it's not an easy shot."

"And you have to do that from right there?"

"How else could I see it? Why? Am I distracting you?"

He held my gaze as he took his shot. "No. Not at all."

And...

He made the shot.

Jerk. Some guys just can't be ruffled that easy.

I would've probably challenged him to best of five and upped the flirting another notch but just as I was turning to order another round from Abe a tall guy with stringy blonde hair walked in.

"Looks like our guy just got here. You want to take this one?" I asked. Even from across the room I could see what Lance had been talking about. The man who'd just walked in did not belong in the Creek Inn. He probably didn't belong anywhere that didn't involve illegal everything or four walls of concrete and some steel bars.

Matt glanced around. There was only one other woman in the whole bar and she was very clearly with a large man with a big beard and big arms. While we'd been playing pool a few guys had been watching us. I wasn't sure if they wanted the table

A Missing Mom and Mutt Munchies

or me, but clearly Matt had his opinions on the matter.

"How about we both go chat with him?"

"Okay. But you take the lead."

CHAPTER 16

The man leaned against the end of the bar as he waited for Abe to pour him a shot of Jack Daniels. He sized up the room with a narrow-eyed look that put my teeth on edge. This was not a nice man, that was clear. Physically he didn't look like he could do harm to anyone, but there was something about the way he stood and the way he looked at people that made me think he'd play dirty and vicious if it came to a fight.

Reminded me of that Jim Croce song about how you don't mess around with Slim.

I didn't see any obvious weapons, but his belt buckle was big enough to do in a pinch.

(A little trick my grandpa had told me about once.)

A Missing Mom and Mutt Munchies

"You sure you want me to come with you?" I whispered to Matt as we approached.

"Absolutely. Easier to keep you safe that way. But stay behind me."

The man focused in on Matt as we came closer, but didn't move from his not-so-casual slouch.

Matt held out a hand. "Matt Barnes. I'm local police around here. And you are?"

The man looked down at Matt's hand and back up at his face, but didn't take the hand. "Ted Little."

Matt crossed his arms but braced his feet shoulder-width apart. I stayed behind Matt's shoulder, ready to move out of his way if things became physical, which I honestly believed was possible.

"So, Ted. What brings you to Creek?"

"Grew up around here."

"Really. I don't recall seeing you before."

Ted smiled. It was not a nice smile. "Been away a while. You know how it goes."

Matt nodded. "And what brings you here tonight? If you don't mind my saying, the Creek Inn doesn't exactly seem like your type of place."

"It's not. But I ran into a friend here last night. Thought I'd come back and see if she was here again. You have a problem with that?" His voice dropped at the end, threatening.

"Nope. Free country. Who's the friend?"

Ted tensed up even though he was still slouched against the wall. "I don't have to tell you."

"True. You don't. But you'd be helping me out a lot if you would. Turns out a friend of ours was in here last night, too. Trish Mullens?"

He grunted. "Huh. Same friend." He flicked a glance back and forth between us. "But you don't look like the type to be friends with a girl like Trish, if you don't mind my saying."

"I coached her son in baseball. Trish made every game. She may have her faults, but she's a good mom. I respect that."

A Missing Mom and Mutt Munchies

Ted's eyes went flat and hard. "Not so sure I agree about her being a good mom. She's shacked up with Vick Kline, isn't she?"

Matt shrugged his shoulders. "Bad taste in men, but she loves her kid. As far as I can see, she's doing the best she can."

"Except she took off again, didn't she? Kid's birthday's tomorrow and where is she?"

I leaned around Matt. "How did you know that? How did you know that Sam's birthday is tomorrow?"

He transferred those black eyes to me and I was suddenly reminded of a cobra about to strike. "Kid's mine."

"Sam's your son?"

"Surprised? Yeah, well, so was I when she told me. **After** I was sent up for arson and couldn't do a thing about it."

Seems Trish was smarter than she looked if she'd kept this man out of her son's life.

Matt nudged me back. "If he's your kid, how come I've never heard anything about you before this?"

141

"I just got out. Was trying to figure out how I was going to handle things. Went to Vick's looking for Trish last night and he said she'd split but might be here, so I came by. Walked in the door and saw her draping herself all over some loser in a polo shirt. Day before her kid's birthday and she's in here trying to pick up some new guy?" He spat on the ground.

The Creek Inn was not the kind of place where you spit on the ground. But Abe just gave me a subtle head shake. No one was looking for trouble with this guy.

"So you pulled her away for a talk." Matt leaned forward slightly, challenging him just a bit.

He sat up a little straighter, returning the challenge. "I did. Someone needed to remind her what her priorities should be."

"And then you roughed her up. Wanted to make the lesson stick."

"Nope."

When Matt just stared at him, Ted leaned forward until his face was inches from Matt's. "That woman is

A Missing Mom and Mutt Munchies

the mother of my child. It's his birthday tomorrow. I wasn't going to hurt her because that would hurt him. And I don't need fists to get my point across. Trish heard what I had to say and then she got out of here just like I told her to."

I leaned around Matt again. "So you guys just talked then?"

"Yeah, we just talked."

"In here?" I was hoping to trip him up. Catch him in a lie.

"No. Out in the parking lot. Where it was quiet enough for her to hear what I had to say."

I swallowed, not liking to have his attention on me, but wanting to get all the information I could out of him. "And what exactly did you have to say?"

"That she needed to get home to her kid. And that I was back and I was going to be a part of his life from here on out so she'd need to be sure she kept his best interests in mind. Or else."

"What did she say to that?"

He laughed softly. "She didn't appreciate my interfering in her life.

Aleksa Baxter

It seems I'm a no-good loser who doesn't know the first thing about being a father. That I couldn't help out before so what made me think I had the right to be part of his life now."

"And you didn't do anything when she said that?"

"Like I said. My kid's birthday's tomorrow. He doesn't need to have his mom all black and blue in all the photos. Been there, done that myself."

"And she wasn't beat up already?"

"No."

"What happened then?"

"She left. Called me a bunch of names as she was storming towards her car and then tore out of here and headed back towards town. You're awfully full of questions. What's **your** name?"

I opened my mouth to answer, but Matt interrupted, "Thanks for your time. Appreciate it."

He led me straight outside. I didn't even have time to wave goodbye to Abe before we were out the door and headed for his truck.

A Missing Mom and Mutt Munchies

"What did you do that for?" I asked.

"Get in, Maggie."

"But..."

"Get in." He held the door for me and waited until I was seated and buckled in before going around to the driver's side. I could see Ted Little standing in the doorway of the Creek Inn, watching us.

"What's wrong?" I asked as Matt got into the driver's side and started up the truck.

He held up a hand as he dialed his phone. When the person on the other end of the line answered he said, "Hey, it's Matt. Ted Little? That the guy I think it is? The one who went away for burning down the house of a guy he'd had a fight with? Mmhm. Yeah, well, he's out and back in town. Figure it won't be long until you're dealing with him again. At the Creek Inn right now. Yep. Gotta go."

He hung up and pulled out onto the highway. "That man in there is a vicious criminal. The last thing you need to do is get on his radar, Maggie."

"Granted, he's not someone I'd invite over for Sunday dinner, but..."

"Maggie. Ted Little went away for arson, but he was suspected of a lot more. There were three women who went missing while he was around. The disappearances stopped when he was sent away. Cops always figured he'd done it, but no one could find them and no one was talking back then. Until he's back in jail I want you to be very careful. No walking Fancy unless I'm with you or your grandpa is."

"Don't be ridiculous. What does that man care about me?"

"I'm not." He was so serious, the smile dropped from my face.

"Look, I'm sure I'll never cross paths with him again. I mean, it's not like he and I are going to be running in the same circles. And do you really think he'd risk getting bit by a big dog like Fancy when there are easier targets out there?"

"Fancy? Fancy who loves all men and wags her tail and snuggles up against anyone who rubs her ears? She's not a good guard dog, Maggie.

A Missing Mom and Mutt Munchies

Maybe if it was Hans I'd feel differently, but Fancy is not going to protect you from the likes of Ted Little."

There was no point in arguing with him about it. A few weeks would pass, he'd forget about it, and I could go back to living my life like I wasn't surrounded by dangerous killers. He was a cop. He should know that most people do violence to people they already know.

"He's probably the one who took Trish, you know," I said to change the subject.

Matt shook his head. "No. I don't think so. If he'd hurt Trish last night he wouldn't be at the Creek Inn today. It's not his kind of place. Only reason he'd be back there again tonight was to make sure she wasn't."

"I guess that makes sense. So now what?"

"Now I take you home. You tried, Maggie. You talked to Vick, you called her mom and friends, you talked to the city boy, you talked to Ted. There's nothing left to do."

Aleksa Baxter

I stared out the window as we wound our way through the canyon, even though it was pitch black and I couldn't see a thing. Why they'd never bothered to put lights in the canyon I'd never understand. And why the most popular bar in the valley was on the other side of that canyon...Yeah, that didn't make a lot of sense to me either.

"I can't just let it go, Matt."

"Well, you come up with some other idea of where Trish is, you let me know. But for now I think you're done."

He was right. I'd exhausted all my leads. But I wasn't ready to quit.

I had to find Trish. For Sam.

CHAPTER 17

I didn't sleep well that night. Not at all. The house was completely silent. Matt and Jack had taken Sam home with them and my grandpa was still over at Lesley's when I went to bed. Being alone in that big house gave me the jitters.

And since I'd built those stairs for Fancy I rarely had a perfect night's sleep. She'd sprawl so far across the bed that I was left with a narrow strip across the very top. The only thing that saved me from falling off onto the floor was the headboard. I could've probably pushed her to the bottom half of the bed but she was just too darned cute when she started doing that snuffling cry thing in her sleep.

But the real issue was the job offer from Karen.

I knew Jamie. She'd never just walk away from the café and leave me in the lurch. She wasn't that type of person. So as much as she might talk about living in Paris with Mason, she wouldn't do it. Not as long as we were running a business together.

But was it honestly fair of me to ask that of her? I knew we both loved parts of running the place. Being in charge for once and being able to choose who we worked with was a big part of what I loved about it. And living where we both wanted to live.

I also knew, though, that Jamie was sick and tired of making the same thing every day and there was no chance she'd be able to get away from making cinnamon rolls anytime soon.

Sure, we could hire staff, but that's the worst thing to do when you're a brand new business and can do the work yourself. Better to do things ourselves and fund it with our sweat equity. Plus, no employee will care as much as the owner.

A Missing Mom and Mutt Munchies

Oh, some people come close because that's just who they are, but when it's your business...It's a whole different level of care and concern.

They always say to figure things will cost twice as much, take twice as long, and earn half as much as you plan. And so that's what we'd planned for. But it was still going to take twice as long and cost twice as much as **that**.

Wasn't it better to just take Karen's offer and let Jamie off the hook so she could move on with Mason and whatever exciting plans they'd made? At least one of us would be happy.

And then there was my grandpa. He said he didn't need me. And he certainly acted like he didn't need me. But if I went back to DC how many dinners and casual conversations would I miss? There was no amount of money on this planet to make up for that. Was there?

Because what if I said no to Karen now and three years from now she said it was too late to come back there. I'd be without the barkery and without a career.

Aleksa Baxter

Of course, I might lose all those dinners anyway now that things had changed with Lesley. I wouldn't be surprised if my grandpa pulled out his old battered RV and took to the road with her for a while. Out of sight out of mind, you know.

And what about Fancy. I knew she'd go along with anything. I'd already dragged her halfway across the country once and she'd settled into her new normal just fine. She'd do it again if she had to. But what was best for her? Being with me or my grandpa all day or going to some day care with a bunch of other dogs? I think she liked having a yard, but maybe she'd preferred taking walks with me three or four times a day if that also meant getting to play with other dogs more.

Of course, when she'd been in day care they told me most afternoons after her lunch break she'd refused to go back to the playroom, preferring to stay by herself instead.

And then there was Matt.

The best thing for him was for me to leave so he didn't miss some great opportunity at love and happiness

A Missing Mom and Mutt Munchies

that was right there in front of him because he was too busy thinking he could make something happen with me. (I just knew if I wasn't there he'd quickly find a wonderful woman who'd love him for the amazing man he was. She'd probably even like cleaning the house and doing laundry.)

But it was hard to walk away from that potential. There was something there whether I wanted there to be or not. And no amount of fighting it would change that fact.

Not that I'd ever go there...

Disgusted with myself and my inability to know what I wanted out of life after thirty-six frickin' years on this planet, I stared at the ceiling and tried to distract myself with thoughts of Ted Little, Vick Kline, and Trish Mullens.

Had Trish gone back home? Had Vick done something to her when she did? If so, why hadn't there been any sign of it? Vick didn't strike me as the sharpest blade in the drawer. Or had Ted Little done something to her? He did strike me as smart enough to go back to the Creek Inn the next night to give himself an alibi. And nasty enough to have harmed her. Both of those men did.

Honestly, you'd think you cross paths with one man like that you figure out how not to do it again, but like my grandpa had said, I'd never been there so I shouldn't judge. Maybe you chose one to get away from the last one and just kept on making bad decisions on down the line until you forgot there was anything better out there than what you had. Or until you got so scared of what might come next you figured the devil you knew.

Finally, I gave up on falling asleep and pulled out the book I'd been dying to read. Fancy took herself to the living room when I turned on the light, clearly indicating with her disgusted departure exactly what she thought of humans who turn on bedroom lights in the middle of the night.

🐾 🐾 🐾

I'd only been reading for a few minutes when my grandpa came home.

A Missing Mom and Mutt Munchies

"Maggie? What are you still doing up?"

"Just have a lot on my mind."

I told him what we'd found at the Creek Inn.

He shook his head. "Ted Little's back, huh? That's a man you wish would've been shivved in the shower. If I'd known you'd be here at the same time as him I might've tried to arrange it myself."

"Grandpa!"

"He's a bad man, Maggie. You..." He settled himself on the edge of the bed and looked at me. "You've never truly seen evil. I have. In prison, some guys are just in there trying to do their time and get out and get back to their lives. Some make mistakes that they regret almost immediately. But others...They're proud of what they've done. They relish hurting other people. They don't see someone like you as human or worth protecting. You're prey."

I wanted to roll my eyes at what he was saying, but I knew every single word was deadly serious. My grandpa didn't talk about his time in prison often, but when he did it always was.

"I already promised Matt I'd keep away from him. We have no reason to cross paths."

"Doesn't mean he won't find you. Listen to Matt on this one. Don't go out alone until Little is back in prison."

This time I did roll my eyes. "I have to drive to work, you know. And run the barkery."

"I know. Just...Be as safe as you can, Maggie May. Please."

"Fine. I will."

"So that's what had you up in the middle of the night? Not being able to find Sam's mom?"

I shook my head and told him about the call from Karen. I'd tried very hard not to talk to my grandpa about the kind of money I was earning in DC because it was so foreign to how we'd grown up and what most of the people I knew were used to, but I couldn't get his advice if I didn't tell him what I was dealing with. So I told him what she'd offered.

A Missing Mom and Mutt Munchies

"For all three years?"

"Nope. That's per year. And they're going to pay housing and doggie day care for Fancy on top of it."

"So after three years you'll have earned..."

"Yep." My stomach clenched because I knew what he was going to say.

"You have to take it, Maggie May. You can't walk away from that kind of opportunity."

"But...you. And the barkery. And..."

"Maggie May, how many times in your life is someone going to offer you money like that?"

I clenched my pillow to my chest. "Probably never again."

"Exactly. Take it." He patted my leg and stood up. "And now I better get to bed because I am not used to being up this late anymore and I need my beauty sleep."

He turned off my bedroom light as he left, but I didn't fall asleep immediately. I'd been leaning towards taking the job because it made the most sense, but when he

Aleksa Baxter

told me to take it all I could do is feel this dropping sensation in my stomach. Like I was walking away from my only chance at having the life I wanted.

Sure, I'd have money. Enough money to go heli-hiking, that's for sure. But what would I lose that had nothing whatsoever to do with money?

With that happy thought, I finally drifted off to sleep.

CHAPTER 18

As much as I wanted to find Sam's mom, I unfortunately had a business to run, too. So even though the disappointment I knew I'd see in Sam's big brown eyes haunted me, Trish couldn't be my priority. Especially if I was going to leave soon. I owed Jamie more than that.

    I gave up on taking Fancy in with me when she pulled out of her collar for the third time as I tried to drag her out of the backyard. I gave her a stern lecture to leave the bunnies alone before I left, though. Not that she was going to listen, but fortunately they were all faster than her. At least the ones that ran were. I hoped they'd all learned the "don't freeze near the big black dog" lesson when bunny number one went down.

Aleksa Baxter

I didn't tell Jamie about the offer. I wasn't going to tell her about it until I'd figured out which way I was going to go. No need upsetting her one way or the other until I knew if it was an actual option for me.

I was in back dealing with some online orders when someone rang the bell for the barkery counter. Usually if we're slow Jamie will hop over and catch any customer while I'm in back, but it was still a pretty busy time for us on the café side, so I rushed out to see who it was before she had to try to juggle both at once.

Ted Little leaned against the counter with that same predator's slouch he'd had the night before at the Creek Inn. Only a fool would miss just how dangerous he was.

I stopped about a foot away from the counter. "Mr. Little. This is a surprise."

"Isn't it, though?" He glanced down at the bakery display case where I had barkery bites and doggie delights showing. "People pay for this sort of thing, huh? Dog treats priced like chocolate truffles."

A Missing Mom and Mutt Munchies

"Yes. Some people do. You have a dog, Mr. Little?"

"Oh, call me Ted." He smiled at me and I wished my grandpa and Matt were right behind me, one on each side.

"Ted then. You have a dog, Ted?"

"No."

"Then how can I help you." If it had been anyone else there would've been a lot more bite in my words. But the last thing I wanted was to trigger him to take more of an interest in me than he already had.

He stood up straighter. "I think we should become friends. You and I could get along real nice."

Every instinct in my body was screaming at me to run away. Now.

But I'd long ago decided that I wasn't going to let anyone use fear to intimidate me or force me to do something I wouldn't do otherwise, so instead I looked him in the eye. "Hate to disagree, but I don't think you and I have all that much in common."

He pressed his hands into the glass on the counter as he leaned forward. "We could."

Jamie was just feet away helping café customers. I could shout for her and she'd come running. But I didn't need to give Ted Little another target. Having me was bad enough. Plus, he wasn't actually doing anything other than being incredibly intense and scary.

I crossed my arms and leaned against the wall. "You know, Matt believes what you told him last night. That you didn't take Trish. That you didn't hurt her."

"But you don't?"

"I think you're a smart enough man you could have taken Trish and come back the next night to give yourself an alibi."

He chuckled. "That would be mighty convoluted of me, don't you think?"

"Maybe. Maybe not."

His grin vanished as he stared at me with those black, black eyes of his. "I didn't hurt Trish. Like I said before. She's my son's mother and I'm not going to do something like

A Missing Mom and Mutt Munchies

that on the day before my boy's birthday."

He looked me up and down, a slow smile spreading across his face. "But you on the other hand..."

I did my best to hide how much he scared the living daylights out of me. If I shuddered in front of him, I knew I was gone. Whether it was in that moment or some other moment, he'd eventually come after me.

Fortunately, Matt walked in the door just then. I saw his hand go to where his gun would normally be if he was in uniform.

"Matt. Be right with you," I called, forcing a smile on my face. "Can I get you anything else, Mr. Little?"

Ted Little turned and leaned his elbows on the display case as Matt approached. "What do we have here? Well if it isn't the friendly officer from last night." He stood up, glancing back at me. "Thank you for your time, Miss Carver. Sometime soon we'll have to get to know each other well enough you can just call me Ted."

As he strolled out, brushing shoulders with Matt, I saw Matt's hands clench into fists. I fully expected Matt to clock him one, but he didn't. What he did do is turn and watch until Ted got in his old gray sedan and drove away.

Only then did he turn towards me.

I stood with my hands braced on the edge of the counter, trying to catch my breath.

Only one other time had I felt that sort of primal fear that makes you shudder against your will. It was watching one of those shows on serial killers. I can't remember which one, there are so many. But this one had footage of an interview with the actual killer. It wasn't a re-enactment. It was real live footage. And when that man spoke...I'd had this visceral, gut-deep reaction to him. Thousands of years of evolution screaming in my mind to run and hide even though the footage was twenty years old and the man was on my television.

"You okay?" Matt asked.

A Missing Mom and Mutt Munchies

"I will be once that man is back in prison. Or dead." I shook myself until the feeling went away. "I need a Coke. Only because it's too early for a straight shot of whiskey. You want one."

"Sure. That'd be great."

As I grabbed us both a Coke, Matt studied me. "I didn't know you drank whiskey."

"I don't. Other than an unfortunate period of time when I thought it was cool to drink Malibu rum straight up, I've never been much of one for hard alcohol. I figure that's taking your drinking way too seriously. But this would've been symbolic."

He chuckled, but we were both still on edge and we knew it.

CHAPTER 19

Matt stuck around for a bit, but he eventually had to leave. He made me promise before he left that I'd call him if I saw Ted Little again.

"It's a small town, Matt. How many times a day do you want me to be calling you?"

"As many as you need to. I don't care if you see him when you're at the grocery store, Maggie. You call me."

"So you can what? Run over there and glare at him?"

"Just call me, Maggie. Please."

"Fine. But better be prepared to hear from me a dozen times a day."

I knew it was a good idea. I knew that for whatever reason Ted Little had fixated on me. But what can I

A Missing Mom and Mutt Munchies

say? When I'm scared I become obnoxiously sarcastic.

After Matt left I kept wondering if Ted Little was the reason Trish was missing. I had no doubt he was capable of murder. None whatsoever. But he seemed sincere when he talked about not ruining Sam's birthday. And it was pretty convoluted for him to go back to the Creek Inn the next night just to establish an alibi when probably no one knew he was out of prison.

He was an option, about the only option we had, but not a clear-cut one.

🐾 🐾 🐾

Business on the café side was steady throughout the rest of the morning. The barkery side, not so much.

A woman did come by and ask if we had boarding available, but I had to tell her no. She wasn't the first who'd done so. Early on I'd had to actually put up signs over the cubbies along the wall informing people that no, they could not just walk in and leave their dogs for a couple hours while they went for a hike. The cubbies were for when someone wanted to bring their dog but not have them at the table. Or for when they ran to the bathroom real quick. Not as some unsupervised drop-off doggie day care.

Since I had nothing better to do, I spent most of my time contemplating Karen's offer.

Finally, I couldn't wait anymore. Our lunch rush was almost over and we still had someone in to watch the counter so I dragged Jamie out back with me. She hadn't brought Lulu to work—she said Lulu preferred to stay at her mom's house where she had full access to the backyard all day but I wondered if it wasn't just part of pulling away from the business—so it was just the two of us.

Jamie sprawled on the bench against the wall and wiped a hand across her flour-dusted forehead as I stared out at the distant mountains.

"Phew. It's nice to get out and see the sun for a bit. I swear, I'm cooped up in that kitchen so much I almost forget how enjoyable summers can be here." She took a long drink of water. (Unlike me, Jamie actually

A Missing Mom and Mutt Munchies

worries about her health and her figure.)

I paced towards the stream and back. "That's kind of what I wanted to talk to you about."

I couldn't bring myself to sit, so I loomed over her, my arms crossed.

"What? What's wrong? Sit down, you're scaring me."

I shook my head. I couldn't sit down.

I turned away. It was so beautiful with the mountains rising in the distance and the stream and the trees. (If you forgot that there had very recently been a dead man found in those trees...) There were birds singing somewhere and it was quiet enough you could actually hear the water burbling along. And it smelled so crisp and clean. So pure.

I loved it. I loved it so much.

And it was nothing at all like DC. But...

I bit my lip and turned back around. I didn't want to cry. This wasn't bad. Not for Jamie, at least.

Not even for me, really. (So why did it feel so bad?)

"Jamie, look. I, um..."

"What is it?" She leaned forward, studying my face, ready to leap to her feet and solve whatever the issue was like the ultra-competent friend she was.

"Um. Karen called me last night."

"Karen? As in your old boss, Karen?"

I nodded.

"What did she want?" Jamie hadn't been a fan of Karen's since I told her about the time Karen called and woke me up at three in the morning to participate in a two-hour conference call where I hadn't even been needed. When I'd told her about that she'd informed me that anyone who couldn't value their staff more than that didn't deserve staff as dedicated as I was.

I kind of agreed. Especially since Karen had never even acknowledged that participating in that call was anything less than what should've been expected from me.

A Missing Mom and Mutt Munchies

Man, I did not want to go work for that woman again. (And to be fair, it wasn't just her. It was the whole company. Probably the whole industry. Working long hours was some sort of badge of pride. It all came down to how much you earned, who your clients were, how nice your clothes were, and how many hours you worked.)

But my friend deserved to be let out of the situation she was trapped in. She deserved to enjoy a sunny day if she wanted to.

Plus, Karen and her team needed me. They weren't going to get the project without me. And I couldn't let them down like that.

And there was the money. And the fear of failure if I stayed and the barkery went under. That inevitable slide into insignificance.

So, pacing back and forth, I told Jamie about the offer. And about why I was going to take it. About how it would free her up to go to Paris with Mason or to go wherever else she wanted with him, even if that was just home for lunch on a nice summer's day.

"You're the best baker in the world, Jamie, but I also know you hate having to make cinnamon rolls every single day of your life. This...It isn't what we thought it would be."

I almost did cry then. I'd wanted it so bad. To live in a small town in Colorado with my dog and my grandpa and my best friend. To run a silly little business that was anything I wanted it to be. To have something that was completely mine.

But life changes on you. And it wasn't working. Not anymore. Maybe it never had been.

Jamie sat forward, studying me with an intensity that made my skin itch. "You're right, Maggie. It isn't what we thought it would be. And while I do love that people love my cinnamon rolls, I don't want to have to spend the next twenty years of my life getting up before the sun baking them."

I'd been right. I turned away.

"But..." She stood and grabbed my arm, turning me back around to face her. "I am not okay with my best friend moving states away and going

A Missing Mom and Mutt Munchies

back to a career that made her miserable. Maggie, how many weekends did you spend Saturday in the office and Sunday shopping for crap you didn't even need just to make yourself feel better?"

I shrugged one shoulder. "Too many. But less after I got Fancy. I'll be better this time."

"No you won't. You don't have it in you to give less than a hundred percent. And since Karen will ask for a hundred and ten percent you'll end up giving everything. You can't go back there."

"But you agreed. This isn't what we thought it would be. It isn't what either of us want. You can stay because you have Mason now. I have...nothing."

Jamie snorted, a not very lady-like sound for someone I was used to seeing as classy. "Nothing? Your grandpa. Matt. That's nothing?"

"My grandpa has Lesley now. And Matt's probably going to re-enlist."

"He wouldn't re-enlist if you asked him to stay."

I glared at her. "I can't ask him to stay when I know I can't be with him."

Jamie opened her mouth to argue with me but I held my hand up to stop her. "I'm not discussing that with you, Jamie. I love you to death. You're my best friend. But we have very different takes on love and all of that and I'm just not going there. You won't convince me to feel differently than I feel about it so just leave it alone."

She tapped her foot on the ground as she studied me. "Okay. But promise me this. You'll give me two hours before you call Karen and accept this ridiculous offer that she should've never made to you."

"It's not ridiculous. They need me."

"It is, too, ridiculous. You'd gotten out, Maggie. Don't let them pull you back in."

"But the money..."

"Oh, screw the money. Like you care about that. Two hours." She held my gaze. "Promise?"

I nodded.

A Missing Mom and Mutt Munchies

   After she'd run back inside I collapsed onto the bench and stared at the mountains. I loved this place. It was my home. But logic told me taking Karen's offer was the best choice.

CHAPTER 20

I spent the next hour calling all of Trish's friends and family one more time. I even called Abe to see if she'd shown up at the Creek Inn after we'd left or if he'd remembered anything new. But nada. No one had heard from her, no one had seen her. It was Sam's birthday and he was going to spend it without his mom because I couldn't figure out what had happened to her.

I hung up the phone—I'd been using our office phone—and stared at all the little to-do lists and checklists on the poster board on the wall. Jamie was nothing if not organized. She had an opening checklist, a closing checklist, and even a checklist for preparing cinnamon rolls. I wondered if after all these weeks of

A Missing Mom and Mutt Munchies

making the rolls every morning she still followed it.

Knowing Jamie, yes. She liked completing tasks. Putting that little x next to each one as it was finished.

She knocked on the doorframe. "You done with your calls?"

I nodded.

"Good. I need to speak with you. Betty went home and I closed up early. But you have to promise me something first."

I frowned at her. "What?"

"You won't be mad at me."

"If you want me to promise you I won't be mad, I can't."

"Why not?"

"Because the fact that you're asking means I'm going to be. And you know me, I'm not exactly good at hiding my emotions."

She nodded. "Good point. Well, just promise me you'll try. Come on. We're set up out front."

I followed her to the front of the store where Greta and Mason were seated side-by-side at one of our larger tables.

Aleksa Baxter

They both looked perfect, as always, Greta in black slacks and a bright blue top, Mason in gray slacks and a black t-shirt I figured cost more than my whole wardrobe. (Which isn't saying much. I'm cheap and I like to buy things that are on sale. It's just clothes. As long as I'm not in danger of being arrested for lewdness I figure I'm covered. Literally and figuratively.)

But they also both looked nervous.

Jamie kissed Mason's cheek and squeezed his shoulder. I had to admit, he was a good-looking man even with his salt and pepper hair. He was one of those men who have presence when they walk into a room. Women always turned to take an extra look and really, who could blame them?

Still. He'd always struck me as a little bit too uptight for my tastes.

That day he was in full-on stick mode, his spine as straight as humanly possible.

I didn't know why they were there, but it felt very much like an ambush.

A Missing Mom and Mutt Munchies

I glanced towards the front door and saw that Jamie really had locked up.

"I thought we weren't going to close early anymore," I said as Jamie ran back to the kitchen for a tray with a Coke for me, coffees for each of them, and a gorgeous cake with delicate white piping.

If you have posted hours you should keep them even if you know no one will come in for the last two hours you're open. Otherwise, why bother staying open that long. All it takes is that one time that person who would've come in on a regular basis at three each day drops by to find you closed to lose them.

"Don't worry. It'll be okay. You're talking about leaving anyway, remember? And if you do that, the fact that we closed two hours early one Monday afternoon isn't really going to make a difference."

"I guess not." I grudgingly sat down at the table as Jamie passed around drinks and sliced up the cake. It was lemon. One of my favorites. "Hi Mason. Hi Greta."

They both said their hellos, but there was still that nervousness to them. Like they thought I was going to suddenly attack them or something. I turned to Jamie. "What's this about?" I snapped.

Greta let out a sound that was part exasperation, part disgust as she passed Hans a small treat that he took with all the dignity of a true gentleman. "Honestly, Maggie. You will find out soon enough, yes?"

Couldn't fault her logic even if it did feel like an ambush. I took a quick bite of the cake. It was delicious. Moist and tangy and just sweet enough. Jamie truly is a genius in the kitchen.

But then I put my fork aside and waited to see who was going to do the talking.

They all looked at each other, none wanting to be the one that started. Finally, Jamie turned to face me. "We were waiting to talk to you about this because we wanted to iron out some final details. To make sure it was going to happen before we sprung it on you. But since you're talking about taking that offer from Karen I

A Missing Mom and Mutt Munchies

figured we better tell you about it now."

"Tell me about what?" I glared at all three of them, my appetite gone.

The thought that the two women I considered my best friends in town and my friend's fiancé had been talking about something important behind my back made me feel ill.

"Remember the two plots of land that Janice Fletcher left? And how Mason had wanted to buy them so he could turn this area into a resort?"

I glared at Mason. "Mmhm. But he didn't buy them. I checked. It was some corporation no one had ever heard of. So we're safe from him tearing down our business and ruining our lives."

"Maggie."

I shrugged one shoulder. "I know you love him, Jamie. But that would've ruined everything."

"Not necessarily."

I narrowed my eyes at her and then looked at Mason and Greta before finally turning my glare on Greta. "It was you? You own the corporation that bought the plots of land?"

She nodded.

"And now you're working together. You and Mason. You're going to build that resort. You're going to tear down the barkery. Well, guess it's good I decided to take that offer of Karen's then, isn't it. Gets me out of the way all nice and neat." I took a sip of Coke but my hand was shaking.

Jamie grabbed my wrist when I set the can back down. "No, Maggie. You've got it all wrong. **We're** going to build the resort. All four of us."

"All four of us? Then why am I the only one that didn't know about this little plan until now?"

She bit her lip. "Because I wanted to give it a little time between the engagement and telling you about this. I didn't want you to think we were doing this because of that."

"But aren't you?"

"No. It's..." Jamie seldom looks flustered, but she was definitely struggling to keep calm and explain things to me in a way that would get through effectively.

She sighed and tried again. "Look, Maggie, we can both agree that this

A Missing Mom and Mutt Munchies

place is far more of the type of work that neither one of us enjoys than we'd anticipated, right?"

I shrugged my shoulders, not wanting to agree with her on anything at that point. What can I say, I'm stubborn when I'm angry.

"But there are parts of it I think we both like. You love coming up with new ideas for dog treats. And I love experimenting with different recipes. And the idea is sound. I really do think there's a need for a place where tourists can go with their pets."

I nodded.

"It could be more, though. So much more. And we can find a way to do the fun parts without having to do the parts we don't like."

"Who says there are parts I don't like?" I crossed my arms and refused to look at anyone at the table. If there was a job to do, I did it. Sure there were some parts I wasn't a great fan of, but...

Jamie laughed. "Come on, Maggie. You know that you and customer service are not a good fit. The customer is not always right in your world."

"Well, yeah, some customers are idiots. Or jerks. And I refuse to let someone use anger to get what they want."

I shook my head. "I don't even know why we're discussing this. You've obviously come up with a plan that doesn't need me. And now I have that offer from Karen. So, great. Tear this place down and build your fancy resort with your fancy husband. I'll go back to my old life and we'll all be just as happy as can be."

"Maggie May Carver. Enough. The reason we are here telling you about this now instead of letting you take some ridiculous job offer that takes you back to DC where you are going to be miserable is because we want you to be a part of it. Now sit back, quit being a spoiled brat, and listen."

I was so surprised to see my normally mellow-mannered friend snap at me that I did exactly that as Mason laid out an architect's rendering of a beautiful resort property.

A Missing Mom and Mutt Munchies

He put on his serious lawyer face as he turned to me. "Here is the plan. We are going to build a pet-friendly resort. Top to bottom. We will have big dog and small dog areas as well as cat areas. Each room will have top of the line sound-proofing. There will be a cat café on one end and a dog barkery on the other. We will offer pet spa services, even acupuncture and chiropractor services, as well as boarding. And there will be a novelty shop that's three times the size of what you have here. Think Dylan's Candy Bar but for pets. High-end everything. Top quality. It will be a pet-lover's dream. Anyone who views their pet as part of the family can take them on vacation just like any other member of the family. Full service, luxury, all-inclusive."

It sounded amazing. Like our little barkery idea on steroids. I leaned back and crossed my arms. "Sounds great, but I still don't understand why you need me."

Greta leaned forward. "We don't need you, Maggie, we want you. You are our friend and you are smart and you will help us run this place."

Mason nodded. "This is the plan. We will buy out your interest in the barkery with an interest in the resort. You will run the barkery, retail store, and online sales for the new resort. As a salaried manager. Starting the day this place closes. Your main role will be strategy and management. We will hire staff for the store and order fulfillment. Jamie will do the same for the cat café and restaurant as well as overseeing the hotel staff. Neither one of you will ever have to man a retail counter again unless you want to. And Jamie won't be stuck in the kitchen all day every day."

"We'll get to work together more, Maggie. And on the parts of things that we actually enjoy doing."

It sounded good, but...

I shook my head. "Look, this is a great idea. You've come up with something brilliant here. I think people will love it. And you'll have made a place that people who love their pets will love to go to. But I'm not like you guys. I'm not...flashy. I'm silly Newfie heads on a sign with a bad script font that no one can read. I'm...this." I gestured at the rest of

A Missing Mom and Mutt Munchies

the barkery with its cheesy but adorable displays that didn't scream luxury no matter how you looked at them. "It's a brilliant idea, but it's not for me. It's you guys."

"Maggie..."

"No. It's fine." I stood up and focused on Jamie. "I was worried about taking that offer from Karen because I didn't want to let you down, even though I knew it was the best thing to let you out of this. But now I know you'll be fine. Now I can take it without feeling guilty."

I glanced at Mason and Greta. "Thank you. Truly. For considering how to include me. I'm sure this will be incredibly successful. But..." I shook my head and turned back to Jamie. "I have to go, okay?"

I raced to grab my purse and get out the door before I lost it.

CHAPTER 21

I didn't know where I was headed, I just knew I needed to get out of there.

You might be wondering why I was so upset. I mean, they'd made space for me, hadn't they? It was probably thanks to Jamie and Greta that the resort was going to be a pet-friendly one that could incorporate the barkery. And they hadn't had to include me even then. Not like I had rights to the idea after all.

It was likely inevitable that the minute Janice Fletcher died the barkery would be torn down to create a resort. I mean, not like Mason was earning high rent on the existing building. Not the kind of money he could earn on a luxury resort.

But it just felt like a betrayal.

A Missing Mom and Mutt Munchies

Like my best friend and my only other real friend in town had been conspiring behind my back. It was **their** idea. Not **ours**. I hadn't been part of coming up with what should be included or not. I hadn't helped with the artist's rendering.

Which is why it felt so horrible. Like I was an afterthought.

It didn't help that Mason was involved. Jamie loved him and I was happy for her, but it was hard enough to lose her to love and marriage. Having him take my business, too, was just that last little bit that pushed me over the edge.

As I drove towards home, trying not to lose it, I reminded myself that it was fine. At least I had the offer from Karen. I'd take that, go back to what I was good at, and leave the people who didn't really need me to their lives.

I barely noticed the beauty of the valley as I sped by. The grass was kind of dried out by that part of the season, but the aspen trees scattered amongst the evergreens on each mountainside colored the world with yellows and oranges and even some reds.

It was a perfect day, too. No clouds in a blue, blue sky. I'd miss it.

Of all the east coast cities I'd spent time in DC was probably the best of the lot when it came to nature and greenery, but it wasn't the Colorado mountains. It wasn't wild. It was cultured and controlled. Everything trimmed and tidied. Nature as backdrop instead of centerpiece.

But it was what it was.

And what other choice did I have?

🐾 🐾 🐾

I stormed in the door at home, wanting desperately to talk to my grandpa about everything. He'd understand. Or if he didn't understand he'd at least listen and give me some practical advice and a knock upside the head.

But as soon as I walked in I saw that he had company. He and Lesley were seated on the worn old goldenrod couch. He had his arm wrapped around her shoulders; she'd clearly been crying.

A Missing Mom and Mutt Munchies

I hate to say it, but Lesley looked terrible. She's usually a very polished woman. She has this beautiful white hair that she pulls back into a flawless bun, but that day the bun was falling apart. And her normal red lipstick looked like she'd smeared it on without checking the mirror. She'd lost a good ten pounds since I'd seen her last and there were dark shadows under her eyes.

She had a pallor to her skin that made me want to tell her to get some rest and good food.

Despite it all, at least she'd still made the effort. Good for her.

Fancy was there, too, and came over to say hi. I rubbed her ear and she leaned into my hip with a contented groan. "Lesley. I'm so sorry about your husband."

"Thank you, Maggie. I appreciate that."

"What are you doing home so early?" my grandpa asked.

"We decided to close up. No customers. Thought I'd get in a hike."

I hadn't actually wanted a hike, but Lesley clearly needed time alone with my grandpa. Plus, it would be good to get out and move. Sometimes I think better when I can be active. It was too hot, though, for Fancy. "You okay with Fancy staying here while I'm out?"

He nodded.

"She give you any trouble with the bunnies today?"

"No. I had a man come out this morning and round them up. He set some traps for the ones he couldn't get, but I expect we'll be varmint free in a day or two."

"Aw, Grandpa. Look at you, choosing the humane option."

He harrumphed. "Figured it was easier to do that than listen to you complain about the poor bunnies for the rest of my life. You sure you're okay?"

"Yeah, I'll be fine. Rough couple of days, that's all. I better get changed."

I threw on some hiking pants, a t-shirt, and my hiking boots, and then slathered on sun screen on any

A Missing Mom and Mutt Munchies

exposed skin. No point in getting burnt if I could avoid it. I topped it all off with a Rockies baseball cap. Not the most hiking-worthy of hats, but at least it shielded my face some.

I threw my new book and a can of Coke in my backpack along with the small first aid kit I always carry and figured I was ready to go. I opened the front door to find Matt standing there, just about to knock. "What are you doing here?"

"Jamie called. Told me you might need someone to talk to."

I was torn between anger at Jamie for interfering in my life and gratitude that Matt was there.

"Well, I don't. I was just about to head out for a hike, actually."

"Then I'll come with you. She said you hadn't eaten lunch yet, so I brought some sandwiches for us. I was going to suggest we take them up to that big rock you like so much."

"How'd you know about that?"

"You'd be surprised what I know. Come on." He stepped back to let me out the door. "Mr. Carver. Lesley." He

193

Aleksa Baxter

nodded at them before closing the door firmly behind me.

CHAPTER 22

We walked up the mountainside in silence, picking our way towards the large rock on the side of the mountain that I'd always considered my true home. It was harder to get to now that Mr. Jackson was gone. While he was alive he'd kept the trail that led up the mountainside nice and trimmed (so he could reach his pot stash), but now it was largely overgrown.

Forcing my way through helped me work off some of my anger so that I was mostly calm by the time we finally reached the rock and sat down cross-legged to look down on the town of Creek.

It might not be much to look at, but I loved the view anyway.

"What did you bring?" I asked Matt as he opened up his backpack. As far as I knew the only things he ate at home were fast food, burgers cooked on the grill, and cans of tuna fish.

"A couple of sandwiches. Turkey and cheddar with tomatoes, lettuce, and mayo. I remembered you don't like mustard. And a bag of chips and a couple of apples, too."

"Not bad."

"I try." He grinned at me and my heart gave a little tug, taking the last of the anger with it.

I didn't want to be mad at Matt. He didn't deserve it. He hadn't betrayed me. And he hadn't made me an offer I couldn't refuse but desperately wanted to. His only fault was that he was such a good person I couldn't just write him off.

I pulled out my Coke and cracked it open.

"Water's better for a hike, you know."

"Yeah, well, I often do what isn't the best for me."

A Missing Mom and Mutt Munchies

He let that go and we sat in silence as we ate our sandwiches. Finally, Matt said, "Nice view."

"It is, isn't it? One of my favorite places in the world. I used to come up here in the summers and count the number of cars in each of the freight trains that passed by."

"Me, too."

"From here?"

"No. From my dad's place. There's this little spot right at the edge of our property that's good for fishing. I used to sneak down there as often as I could. This was before we moved, of course. I could see the train tracks from there and I'd count the cars as they went by."

We sat there for a moment in silence, both of us looking down on the town of Creek. It's not a big town. There are maybe forty houses in the whole town and half of those started off as mobile homes. There's the creek running along the edge of town, the ballpark, the county seat, and the shiny new library building at the edge of town and that's about it. But it's beautiful. And it's peaceful.

And it's home.

I sighed. "I love this town."

"Me, too."

"But you're thinking of leaving." I glanced at him sideways.

He finished his bite of sandwich before answering. "So are you. Aren't you? That offer you got last night?"

"Yeah. They need me."

"Doesn't Jamie need you, too?"

"No."

I told him about the resort offer and how it was clear Jamie, Mason, and Greta had been working on it for a while without me.

"Sounds like they'd planned for you to be involved."

"But they don't **need** me to be involved. Karen on the other hand said they won't get that project without me. So if I don't go back to DC I cost all those people I used to work with a lot of money. I'd rather be needed than some charity case."

"Hm."

"What's that mean?"

"Nothing. It's your choice. But maybe give it another day. Let your

A Missing Mom and Mutt Munchies

temper cool before you make your final decision."

"My temper?" I asked as I felt the anger flare back to life.

He nodded, not looking away or down which is what most people do when I'm in that kind of a mood. It made it a little hard to sustain when he refused to let it affect him.

I crumpled up the paper towel I'd used as a napkin. "I need to walk this off. You up for more of a hike?"

"Sure. But, Maggie?"

I glanced at him. "Yeah?"

"People here, they need you, too. More than you think they do. Just remember that when you're making your decision. Now, come on. There's a gorgeous spot right at the edge of the canyon where you can see for miles on a day like this." He held out his hand and I took it, letting him pull me to my feet.

CHAPTER 23

It only took us about ten minutes to reach the spot Matt had wanted to show me. I liked hiking with him, he kept his pace steady but didn't leave me behind when the altitude (and probably my choice of beverage) made me slow down a bit.

And he was right. It was a gorgeous spot. Breathtaking as a matter of fact.

Off to the right I could see the entire valley stretching off into the distance, the mountains rolling along like they'd never end. It was just...stunning.

To the left was the canyon. I couldn't see as much of it as I could of the valley because of how it twisted and turned. But there was still the sky and that feeling of being

A Missing Mom and Mutt Munchies

part of something larger than myself. Something so powerful I could barely wrap my mind around it.

I closed my eyes, took a deep breath, and let it wash over me.

"Can you really walk away from this?" Matt asked, standing close enough that I could feel the heat of him.

"Can you?" I answered. I sat down cross-legged and stared out into space.

I didn't want to leave. I didn't want to do that work anymore. I didn't want to put Fancy in day care every day. And I didn't honestly care about the money no matter how much it was.

But they needed me. And one of my biggest weaknesses is my inability to say no when someone really needs my help. Like Karen did.

Matt sat down next to me, our knees almost touching. The silence stretched between us for a long moment and then he said, "You know, there's another way to think about what you told me earlier about Jamie, Mason, and Greta."

Aleksa Baxter

"Is there?"

"There is. Instead of thinking about what you're going to lose with the barkery being torn down, you should think about the fact that Greta and Mason, two people who didn't have to make room for you in their lives if they didn't want to, have decided to do so. Think about how you came here to open a business with one person, Jamie, and how you made enough of an impact in that short period of time that both Greta and Mason want you to be part of this amazing resort they're building."

I pressed my lips together.

"And your grandpa? He doesn't show it, but he loves having you here. Sure, Lesley will probably be a much bigger part of his life going forward, but nothing can replace you. You're his only granddaughter. Having you around makes him proud."

"He thinks I should take the project in DC."

"He thinks you should have a life. And he doesn't want to be the one

A Missing Mom and Mutt Munchies

who holds you back from that. Did you tell him about the resort offer?"

"No. I didn't get a chance to. Lesley was there when I came home."

"So he doesn't know that you have a perfectly good choice here, too. Maybe if he did he'd change his mind." He nudged me with his shoulder. "Do you really want to give this up? For any amount of money?"

I made a small pile of pebbles and knocked it back down. "It's not about the money. If I don't go, they won't get the project."

"Too bad. If they can't convince that company to hire them anyway, then that's on them." He leaned close and I could smell the faint hint of aftershave. "Maggie, it might not be as obvious, but the people here need you just as much as those people back in DC. Maybe more."

Our eyes met.

It was one of those moments. One of those moments where that potential between two people can tip over into something more. The possibility hung there between us as

I met his eyes. Eyes so blue I could drown in them.

All it would take was opening up to him. Leaning forward. Letting our lips touch.

That's all it would take...

But I turned away. "We better get back. I still haven't found Sam's mom." I didn't look at him as I stood up and dusted off my pants.

It would've been better if he'd gotten mad at me. If he'd called me on it. But he didn't. He wasn't that type of person. He just quietly started back down the trail.

I paused and took one last look at the view. It really was stunning.

I was going to miss it.

🐾 🐾 🐾

I hated the distance that had suddenly grown between me and Matt. A distance I'd created by turning away.

I knew why I'd done it, but he didn't. He just knew he was this good guy who couldn't get the girl he liked and he probably thought it was about him when it absolutely wasn't.

A Missing Mom and Mutt Munchies

I hurried to catch up to him.

"You know, when I was little Tina's mom would walk us to the center of the canyon for fresh spring water. It bubbled out of this little spot in the canyon wall and we'd take one of those plastic jugs with us and fill it up. Tasted so sweet. So pure. Better than anything you can get with even the best filter."

He nodded, but didn't look back at me. "I remember that. She'd take me along sometimes, too."

"Probably be suicide to do that now, there's enough traffic through the canyon these days I'd never let a kid walk through there. You just never know when someone will veer off the road that little bit."

I carefully stepped over a large rock before adding, "You know I always admired her for having such confidence even though her leg was all mangled up from that car accident. Never let it stop her, though."

"That accident..." Matt stopped so suddenly I almost ran into him. He turned to look at me. "It was in the canyon, wasn't it? Their car rolled down the canyon."

"Yeah. Probably only reason they survived is how drunk they were. At least that's how I heard it."

"That's it."

"What's it?"

He grabbed my shoulders, grinning like a fool. "Trish was driving back from the Creek Inn. **Through** the canyon. Late at night. In the dark. Probably upset because her kid's worthless father just got out of prison and wants back in his life. All it would take is missing one curve."

"You think she drove off the edge?"

"Could've. It's worth looking at."

"Wouldn't someone have noticed?"

"There's no guardrail. So what is there to notice? People zip through there so fast no one's going to see a tire track on the side of the road and think someone went off the side. And there's nothing at the base of the canyon except for the river and the train tracks."

"A train could see her."

A Missing Mom and Mutt Munchies

"There's some switch issue. Hasn't been a train through in days."

I nodded. "It makes sense. And she isn't anywhere else." I gave him a hug. "Quick thinking. Come on. Let's go see if you're right."

I raced down the mountainside, Matt on my heels.

CHAPTER 24

I wanted to go straight to Matt's truck, but I was in desperate need of another Coke by the time we got to my grandpa's, so I veered towards the house instead. As I walked through the front door I saw that Jack and Sam were there working the puzzle they'd started the day before. They almost had it done.

A cute, bright package with little dumpster trucks sat at the end of the table.

"Where'd that come from?" I asked.

"I brought it. It's Sam's birthday after all, isn't it, buddy?" He ruffled Sam's hair. "I thought we could throw him a little party here. Your grandpa said it would be okay."

My grandpa joined us from the direction of his workroom. It seemed

A Missing Mom and Mutt Munchies

Lesley was gone. "He even brought a cake."

I eyed Jack like I'd never seen him before. "Well look at you, Mr. Fine and Upstanding Citizen. Who knew that all it took was one little kid to turn you around?"

"I'm not little." Sam frowned at me. "You found my mom yet?"

"I'm working on it. Matt and I were just about to go check something out actually."

"What?" For a little kid Sam had quite the in-your-face attitude.

"Well, your mom was at a place called the Creek Inn the night she went missing. It's on the other end of the canyon. We thought maybe she'd had an accident coming back home. Missed a turn in the road."

Jack stood up. "You think she rolled her car down the canyon."

"Maybe."

He glanced down at Sam. "You think you'll be okay here with Lou, buddy? I'd like to go help them look."

"Can I come?"

"No."

Aleksa Baxter

It was a good thing Jack had to be the one to tell that kid no, because I would've probably caved and let him come along. But Jack was right. If she'd rolled her car down the canyon, chances were she was going to be in rough shape. (If she was still alive.) No need for Sam to be there when we found her.

Sam pouted, but Jack waited him out. "So you okay staying here?"

"Fine."

"And you okay looking after him for an hour or so?" he asked my grandpa.

"You can help me finish the puzzle," Sam added.

My grandpa snorted, but he nodded his head and sat down in the chair Jack had vacated.

"Then let's go."

"Just give me a second to get a Coke would ya?" I said, heading for the kitchen.

Jack didn't look too pleased to have to wait that whole thirty seconds, but he didn't say anything.

A Missing Mom and Mutt Munchies

Matt did, though. He called after me. "A bottle of water would be better. Grab me one, too?"

Rather than argue especially when I knew he was right, I grabbed three bottles of water. But I did mutter a few choice words about interfering men as I handed Jack and Matt their bottles on the way out the door.

As we piled into the truck, me in the front passenger seat, Jack in the seat directly behind me, I looked at Matt. "What are you thinking? What's the best way to do this?"

"I say we drive through the canyon and you two keep an eye out for any signs that a vehicle went off the edge. If we don't spot anything on the first pass then we'll park and walk back through on foot just in case."

I had no desire to walk through that canyon on foot. Walking along the side with the canyon wall would be scary enough. Walking on the side with the sharp drop off? Ugh. Not worth considering.

Aleksa Baxter

I was so nervous about finding Trish I kept twisting and untwisting the cap on my water bottle until Matt finally reached over and put his hand on mine long enough to get me to stop.

He took his hand back when we reached the canyon and I turned to focus all my attention on any sign of a car going over the edge.

It wasn't much of an edge. In some spots there was no more than a foot or two of loose dirt between the asphalt of the road and open air. There were two, maybe three pull outs in the canyon, but they were all on the other side up against the canyon wall.

Trish would've been coming from the other direction, but at night it would be easy enough to miss a turn and go across a single lane and off the edge. No lights. No guardrail. To think we all drove through that canyon like it was nothing...

I wasn't exactly sure what to look for but I figured it was one of those situations where I'd know it when I saw it.

A Missing Mom and Mutt Munchies

The speed limit through the canyon was only forty miles per hour, but that didn't keep the locals and visitors from winding their way through the canyon at a much less reasonable sixty on most days. Since Matt was probably doing thirty-five he had a long line of angry people piled up behind him and nowhere for them to go.

Someone in the string of cars behind us honked loudly and Matt's grip on the steering wheel tightened. "Anything yet?"

"Nope. Sorry. You just keep your eyes on the road, though. Jack and I will spot anything there is."

We were almost at the edge of the canyon when both Jack and I cried out at the same time.

"That looks promising," I said.

"Definitely. Find a place to park Matt and we'll go back and check it out."

Matt sped up to reach the end of the canyon since that would be the closest place to pull over. You could almost hear the cheers from the cars behind him.

Aleksa Baxter

The road curved over a small bridge at the end of the canyon and just past that there was enough space for a single vehicle to pull over—a scenic viewpoint that fortunately didn't have anyone in it at that particular moment. We piled out of the truck and lined up along the bridge rail to see if we could spot Trish's car, but the canyon curved before the spot where we'd both seen sign someone might have gone off the edge.

Watching the traffic whiz by I did not want to walk back into that canyon, not even a hundred feet. Especially since we'd have to do it on the open air side if we had any hope of spotting Trish's car.

Fortunately, Jack had a better idea. He scrambled up the side of the embankment above where we'd parked the truck, the ground giving way beneath his feet. I held my breath until he'd reached the top edge. That put him on the opposite side of the canyon from the road and let him walk along the ridgeline until he could get a view of where the car might be.

A Missing Mom and Mutt Munchies

"Careful, Jack. We don't want to lose you, too."

I'm not even sure he heard me. He was a man on a mission.

Finally, he stopped and crouched down. "I see a car," he shouted down to us. "I think it's Trish's. Call it in, Matt."

Matt didn't have signal on his phone. Before I could offer him mine, he said, "I'll just drive for help. You stay here."

He hopped in his truck, flipped a U-turn, and drove back towards Creek, leaving me to watch with fear as Jack made his way back down the embankment.

I don't think I managed to breathe until he put his foot down on the side of the road once more.

"You know that's all we needed, you falling into the canyon yourself."

He winked. "Don't worry about me little lady. I have nine lives."

I snorted. "Please. And if you do have nine lives, I'd lay money on the fact that you've used at least seven of them by now."

Aleksa Baxter

"Probably six. But who's counting?"

CHAPTER 25

As we stood there waiting for Matt to come back with the cavalry, Jack said, "Jamie told me why you don't do relationships."

I crossed my arms, suddenly wishing I'd gone with Matt. We didn't need two people standing on the side of the road and I'd rather be with him than having this conversation. Not to mention how angry I was with Jamie for talking about me behind my back. The resort thing was bad enough. This...

This was unforgivable. I knew she meant well, but my issues were no one's business but mine. Of course, Jamie didn't know my reasons, so...

I shook my head. "Nice try. But she can't tell you what she doesn't know."

"She's your best friend. Of course she knows."

"Just because she's my best friend doesn't mean I've had that conversation with her. My general reaction to 'Gee, Maggie, why don't you date someone?' is to say, 'Because I don't want to.' That usually ends the conversation right there. We never get into the hows or whys of it because most people aren't stupid enough to press the point."

I gave him my best death stare, but he just shrugged it off. "You may not have spelled it out for her, but she knows."

"She's wrong."

"I don't know. Makes sense to me. You lose your parents in a car accident and the love of your life in a skydiving accident within a year, it's bound to make you a little gun shy about love."

A wave of fury ran through me. It was not Jamie's business to tell Jack about any of that. It didn't matter if that wasn't my reason for avoiding relationships, it was still personal and none of his concern. But I pushed the

A Missing Mom and Mutt Munchies

anger away because he'd just keep coming at me if he saw it.

I laughed instead. "You think that would shut me down for fifteen years? Lose enough people and that's it? Done forever."

People who know me would've let it drop right then and there. I don't do violence but I certainly know how to lash at someone with my words. Enough for them to back off.

Not Jack though.

"Yeah. I do. Can't be easy to lose so many people you love so close together. And when you're not even out of college."

I took a deep breath and shoved the emotions that were threatening to swamp me back where they belonged.

Death is funny that way. Someone can be gone for ages and then one little comment or one little thing will bring it all right back like it was yesterday. I could go weeks without consciously thinking about my parents or Alex but Jack brings it up and suddenly all I wanted to do was go have a good cry.

I turned to face him, because that was the only way to make him hear what I said. "It wasn't easy. But that's not my issue with relationships." I stepped right up in his face. "And I swear to you, if you tell Matt about this, that that's my reason, I will gut you."

I've never gutted anyone in my life, of course.

I've never punched anyone. I'm pretty sure I've never even slapped anyone. I might've deliberately jostled someone in a crowd once. And I certainly didn't hesitate to use my body to shove a few players around when I played basketball, but overall I don't actually have a violent bone in my body.

In that moment, though, I was absolutely, 100% sincere that I would inflict bodily harm on Jack Barnes if he took those painful moments from my past and used them like that.

And I know it showed.

Jack held his ground, though. The problem with dealing with criminals. They've actually been there and are prepared to take the hit if they have

A Missing Mom and Mutt Munchies

to. "Are you sure? You going to tell me that didn't impact you? That that didn't make you hesitate the next time you met someone?"

I sighed and let go of the anger boiling in my gut.

I wanted to stay angry. Especially with everything that had happened over the last day or so. But I refuse to live life feeling that way. It would eat me up just like battery acid if I let it. So I don't. I feel that rancid feeling building in my gut and I wash it away before it can consume me.

Jack cared about his brother. It wasn't his business, but that's all it was about.

"Yeah, sure. That was a serious double-blow. You know, honestly, I had the exact opposite reaction of what you're thinking when I lost my parents. Losing them is why I fell so hard for Alex. I had this great big gaping hole where they'd been and then I met Alex and BOOM. I was all in. One hundred percent. Right away. Would've been forever, too. But then I lost him. And you know, for a while there it just didn't seem worth the risk to go through that again."

"Exactly. See? I get that. I was head over heels for Trish. Loved that kid, Sam. And then she just left me one day. Tore my heart out. It's not easy to trust like that again."

"But you do eventually. It's what makes us human. It's how we survive. We forget how much it hurt and we try again."

"You haven't."

"No. I haven't. But it wasn't because I lost them."

"Then what was it? Why won't you let Matt in?"

I sighed. "It's not your business, Jack."

"It is, too. Because if he re-ups..."

I closed my eyes. "If he re-ups, that's **his** choice. Not mine."

"He'd stay for you."

I shook my head. "I can't ask him to make a decision like that because of me. He needs to choose to stay here because it's what **he** wants."

"If he does choose to stay, will you let him in?"

"I won't be here. I'm leaving. I got a job offer I can't refuse and they're

A Missing Mom and Mutt Munchies

tearing down the barkery to build a resort." I turned to look down the canyon. "Oh, look who's back."

Matt drove through the canyon with a police car, an ambulance, and a fire truck hot on his heels.

I stepped away from Jack, pretending that I was doing it to make room for everyone to park where they could but really because I wanted to get away from him. It was no one's business but mine why I was the way I was. They just needed to accept that I wasn't going to be like them and leave me to it. How hard was that?

CHAPTER 26

Turns out trying to send someone down into a canyon with sheer walls to figure out if the occupant of a car that went over the side is still alive isn't all that easy.

The emergency vehicles set up a command center across the highway along a rutted service road no one ever used. And then everyone proceeded to gather around and debate the best option for getting down to Trish's car. For thirty minutes.

They discussed having someone repel down the canyon wall where we'd found the tire tracks, but the rock that made up the canyon wasn't the type to rely on for that sort of thing. If they parked a vehicle for someone to anchor to that meant

A Missing Mom and Mutt Munchies

blocking all traffic through the area for as long as that took.

We all knew the horror stories out of Glenwood Canyon every time there was a rock slide there. It was hours and hours to detour around and no one wanted to mess with traffic that way.

Abe and Evan might've appreciated the extra business but we would've been hearing about it for weeks from every single business owner in the valley. Not to mention the horror stories the tourists would spread of how they'd been trapped for hours in the Colorado mountains with nowhere to go.

Live by tourism, die by tourism.

The longer they took to debate things the more agitated Jack became until he stormed off to demand rappelling equipment and a wet suit from one of the mountain rescue guys. The guy would've probably said no and Jack would've probably decked him if Matt hadn't stepped in and vouched for him.

There was some tense back and forth and then the guy handed over

225

his gear and helped Jack set up to lower himself from the edge of the bridge at the end of the canyon.

By the time anyone else noticed what was happening Jack was already over the side and halfway down. He'd taken a headset with him so we all gathered around the speakers in the command tent to listen as he relayed his progress back to us.

Things were no easier at the bottom of the canyon. The river flowed pretty fast through there and half the time there wasn't a bank, at least not on the side where the car had gone over, just the steep-sided canyon and the river. Jack could've crossed to the railroad tracks but then he would've had to risk getting back across to the car once he reached it, which depending on how wide the river was at that point might've been impossible.

Instead he scrambled over sharp rocks and waded through the river, trying to get to Trish without being swept away.

It was slow going and there was lots of creative cussing that I

A Missing Mom and Mutt Munchies

wouldn't want my grandma to hear. It was so colorful at times it might've even made my grandpa blush. (Who am I kidding? Nothing can make my grandpa blush.)

But finally he radioed back that he'd reached the car. He was clearly tense as he said, "Car is on its side. Passenger side is in the water. Driver's side is clear. There's a chance."

We all went silent. No one spoke waiting for the next transmission.

"I'm approaching the vehicle. It's a bit of a scramble here, there's lots of big rocks. I can't see into the car. The windshield is busted up, but still in one piece."

Whatever else he was, Jack obviously still cared for Trish. I could hear it in every strained word.

I didn't even realize I'd done it, but I grabbed Matt's hand and squeezed it tight, praying that Trish had somehow miraculously made it through but knowing she probably hadn't. He squeezed back with just the right amount of reassurance.

"I'm almost there. I..." We could hear it as Jack slipped on a rock and cussed up a blue streak. He was clearly in pain, but he got it together. "I'm lifting myself up now. Looking in the window..."

I didn't even want to breathe.

"I can see her. It's Trish. But she isn't moving."

It had been two days. And she had rolled her car into a canyon. What were we expecting?

I buried my face against Matt's shoulder. I'd wanted to find her. But not like this. What was I going to tell Sam? And what kind of life was he going to have now without his mom? Who would take care of him?

But then...

"She's alive! I tapped on the window and she turned her head to look at me. Get some EMTs down here. Now."

We cheered. Matt hugged me tight and we both laughed with joy. Only for a minute though, because then we had to figure out how to get Trish—who had to be seriously injured—out of that car and to the

A Missing Mom and Mutt Munchies

hospital. She was alive, but if they didn't do things right, she still might not make it.

As the mountain rescue team consulted with the paramedics, Matt and I stood off to the side.

"Should we go home and tell Sam?" I asked. "Or should we stay here and wait?"

He glanced towards the canyon. "I say we wait. Better to do that than go home, tell Sam his mom is alive, and then find out she didn't make it. And...Jack's there."

"Of course. I'd forgotten. Sorry."

He ruffled my hair. "No need to apologize. It's a lot to take in."

We moved ourselves out of the way and settled in to wait, sitting hip to hip in companionable silence.

CHAPTER 27

When it became obvious that it was going to take hours not minutes to get Trish out of the canyon, Matt drove me down the road so I could call my grandpa and fill him in on what we knew so far.

I asked him not to tell Sam.

"The kid's smart, Maggie May. You're not back yet, he knows something's up."

"I know, but...I don't want him to get his hopes up."

"Understood. Hey, you doing okay?"

I shrugged even though he couldn't see it. "Sure. Why do you ask?"

"You seemed awfully upset when you came home earlier. Anything I should know about?"

A Missing Mom and Mutt Munchies

I debated telling him about the resort idea, but I just didn't have it in me to talk about it right then. Instead I asked, "Do you like having me here, Grandpa?"

I'd already decided I was going to take Karen's offer, but I still wanted to know the answer to the question. A "yes, but you're a pain in the patootie" answer would've helped cement things for me.

"What kind of question is that?"

"An honest one."

I could almost see him frowning at me through the phone. "This about that job offer you got last night?"

"That and a few other things. I mean, I moved here to help you out but you don't seem to need it. And now with Lesley, I figure I might just be in the way more than I'm a help. You won't even let me mow the yard."

"Maggie May."

"Well. So, do you like having me here? Or...not."

There was a long silence. My grandpa isn't the most eloquent of men at the best of times and I knew with a question as loaded as the one I'd just asked he'd want to be very careful about what he said.

Finally, he answered. "Maggie May. I don't have any family left other than you. I never had kids of my own. Your dad was as close as I came. And now that he's gone…Well, there's just you. So of course I want you around. You're my only family. And with Bill passing away that just reminds me how precious the ones we love are and how little time we have with them no matter how long that time is."

"Oh." I don't know why, but I hadn't expected him to say that. He's not one for emotion or regret most times.

"But," he added.

"But?"

"But I don't want to be the reason you don't take a once-in-a-lifetime opportunity. That offer you got? The amount of money you're talking. That's not something to pass up. You won't be young and healthy forever. And people won't be making offers like that to you when you're sixty. So

A Missing Mom and Mutt Munchies

as much as I love you and want you to stay around here, I think the best choice you can make is to take that offer. Think about what that money could mean for your future."

"It's just money, Grandpa. Isn't family more important?"

"Depends on how much money you have. When you're broke and can't feed yourself and robbing a bank seems the only option? No. Family is not more important. Not unless they have money to help you out."

I forgot sometimes how rough he'd had it as a kid. Never having been that bad off myself, I couldn't grasp just how bad things can get.

"Maggie May, I know you love that place you started, but, honestly, do you really think it's going to make it?"

"Oh, didn't I tell you? They're tearing it down to build a resort."

"What?"

I told him about the plan Greta, Jamie, and Mason had put together and how they'd made room for me in it but how I also felt like some afterthought add-on they could do without. And, of course, even though they were going to pay me a salary as part of the deal that salary was nothing compared to what I could earn if I went back to DC.

I bit my lip. "So, knowing that, what do you think?"

"I think **you** have to make this choice, Maggie May. No one else can make it for you. I love you. I love having you here. But it seems to me you have a sure thing with that offer in DC. The resort option is better than the barkery. But is it something you can bank your future on?"

A very good question.

I would've talked to him about it further, but my phone beeped to signal an incoming call. It was Karen.

"I've got a call on the other line, Grandpa. Better take this."

"Love you, Maggie May."

"Love you, too, Grandpa."

I thumbed the screen to answer Karen's call. "Hey, Karen. What's up? Thought you were going to give me a couple of days."

A Missing Mom and Mutt Munchies

"I was, but I'm getting a lot of pressure here to let them know if you're in or not. I might lose some team members to other projects if we don't nail this down now."

That's how it always worked there. They made it seem like there was room and flexibility, but there never was.

"Maggie? We need you on this project. You say no, it's going to cost us millions."

I watched Matt sitting next to me, pretending not to listen, but clearly hearing every word.

"It's a big decision, Karen."

"Why? You're wasted there, Maggie. I mean, honestly, a dog bakery? And do you really want to spend the rest of your days in some small town with people who wear overalls and drive pick-up trucks? I mean, come on."

"Actually…yes."

I realized in that moment that what I wanted was to spend my days around people who wouldn't look down on something like that. Small towns and pick-up trucks wasn't all of who I was, but it was a part of me.

And I wanted to be around people who could accept that. Not mock it or dismiss it.

I thought I'd already decided. I thought I was taking the job. But when Karen pushed me I realized that wasn't at all what I wanted my life to be. I'd rather be poor in small-town Colorado, surrounded by my quirky friends and family who weren't perfect but were mine, than in some flash job in DC where I felt like I could only be half of who I was.

Or worse, where I was changing into someone I didn't want to be.

"What did you just say?" Karen asked.

"I can't do it. I can't take the offer. I'm sorry."

"Take a few more days to think about it…"

"No. A few days won't matter. I'm staying here."

"You'd turn this down? Do you know what kind of an opportunity this is?"

"Yeah. One I don't want."

A Missing Mom and Mutt Munchies

"What if we up the hourly rate? I can go up another fifty an hour."

"It's not about money, Karen. It never was. You're just going to have to convince them you can do this without me. I gotta go."

I hung up on her.

I didn't even care if she was upset with me or if I'd burned that bridge and could never go back, because I finally realized I didn't want to go back. Ever.

This was where I wanted to be.

Matt grinned at me. "I knew you weren't going to take it."

"Did you?" I asked. "Because until right then I thought I was."

"Yep. I knew it when you stood there on the edge of the canyon and looked around and your entire face lit up. No way you could walk away from that."

"Well, glad one of us knows me so well."

He just laughed.

CHAPTER 28

They still hadn't brought Trish out by the time I finished my calls, but at least the medics had reached her and gotten an IV into her so she was being hydrated.

After about an hour of debate and back and forth and throwing out more and more absurd ideas they figured out some ingenious plan to get a platform under the car and get it across the river to the railroad side where they could then transport it out of the canyon. It wouldn't have been possible if Trish drove some rugged truck, but she drove a lightweight little compact that four of the guys swore they'd picked up and moved once just as a joke.

(I'd had a car like that once. A Geo Metro. Cheap and reliable, but not all

A Missing Mom and Mutt Munchies

that sturdy. Certainly not a mountain car.)

It took another hour to get everything ready. By then it was starting to get dark in the canyon, but it's not like they could wait until the next day, not with Trish trapped inside.

The whole time Jack stayed by Trish's side. He'd moved the microphone away from his mouth, but I could hear the murmur of his voice as he talked to her, keeping her at ease, letting her know she wasn't alone.

Despite his criminal ways, I had to admit Jack Barnes was a pretty decent guy when he wanted to be.

Finally, they were ready to act. Those of us not down in the canyon huddled around the command center as they coordinated the rescue. It didn't go perfectly. One guy fell in the river and was swept downstream about twenty feet until he managed to rescue himself. He was bruised up but otherwise uninjured.

It also took more than four guys to maneuver the car onto the platform since Trish was inside and they couldn't just tip it over and there was the tiny little matter of a river to deal with. But after a tense forty-five minutes, they had Trish and her car on their way out of the canyon.

From there it was a pretty straightforward rescue. They cut Trish out of the car and loaded her into a helicopter bound for Denver, Jack at her side. She was in rough shape, but still alive. So there was hope.

🐾 🐾 🐾

As Matt and I drove back through the canyon I shuddered to think how Trish had driven off the edge like that and no one had known.

And then to be stuck there, probably trapped, no cellphone signal, knowing her son would think she'd abandoned him on his birthday...

Ugh.

Matt squeezed my hand. "We found her, Maggie. That's what counts."

"You reading my mind again, Mr. Barnes?"

"Maybe." He kept ahold of my hand.

A Missing Mom and Mutt Munchies

I didn't pull it away until we reached my grandpa's. I knew I should, but I just needed that little bit of connection. That knowledge that I wasn't actually alone. That someone might notice I was missing and care enough to find me if something similar happened.

Sam ran out of the house as soon as we stopped moving. "Did you find her?"

I nodded. "We did. But she's not in the clear yet. She was hurt pretty bad."

"Where is she? I want to see her."

"They had to take her to the hospital in Denver. Did you see that helicopter earlier?"

He nodded.

"That was for your mom. Jack's with her. And we'll get you down to see her, but probably not until tomorrow."

He stomped his foot. "Why not? I want to see her now. It's my birthday."

Matt knelt down in front of him. "Your mom was badly hurt. She's going to be in surgery most of the night. There's nothing you can do for her right now and you wouldn't be able to see her even if you were down there. But I'll take you down tomorrow, okay?"

Sam nodded. He wasn't happy about it, but it was what it was.

Fancy started crying her head off, so I went into the house to calm her down. When Matt and Sam eventually joined us I said, "How about some cake? If finding your mom isn't a reason to celebrate, I don't know what is."

"But mom should be here. And Jack, too."

"Tell you what. We'll wait until your mom's better and Jack's here and we'll have a big party for both of you. But this cake isn't going to last that long, so we might as well eat it now."

"Fine." He wasn't that enthused, but I'd seen him eat sweets before. I knew once that slice of cake was in front of him, he'd scarf it right up.

We lit the birthday candles and sang happy birthday to Sam. Even my grandpa joined in and he usually

A Missing Mom and Mutt Munchies

won't, but he at least has a better voice than I do.

"You make a wish?" I asked Sam after he blew out the candles.

He nodded, staring at the cake with an expression much older than his years. If I had to guess, I'd bet he'd wished that his mother would be alright now. That's what I would've wished for. Or maybe that Jack would stick around. That would've been a good choice, too.

Sam may not have wanted to eat cake originally, but once he got started he was all about it. He had three slices and I let him. I figured why not. He'd had a rough enough day and it was his birthday after all. (I had two slices myself.)

I wondered, watching him, if I had blue frosting around my lips the way he did. It was one of those sheet cakes you get from the store that always have that colored frosting that stains everything. With Sam that meant a blue spot on his cheek, one on his nose, stains all over his lips, and on at least four of his fingers. And we all had blue tongues, too. It happens.

Sam might've been a mess, but at least he'd enjoyed it.

We'd been silent as we ate, each of us lost in our own thoughts, but finally Sam set his fork down and turned to me. "You didn't tell me what happened to my mom. Did she run away like Vick said?"

In other words, had she abandoned him on his birthday?

"No. As a matter of fact, she was coming home to you. But she had an accident. Her car went off the road. No one saw it happen so they didn't know she was down there." I squeezed his hand. "If it wasn't for you, we may have never found her in time. It was your faith in your mom that kept us looking. You saved her, Sam."

He started crying and all I could do was let him crawl into my lap and cry himself out. He fell asleep with his head pillowed against my shoulder.

I glanced across the table where Matt was watching us, his expression unreadable.

A Missing Mom and Mutt Munchies

"Since Jack's in Denver, you guys can just stay here tonight if you want," I said.

"That's okay, thanks. We're all set up at my place. Here, I'll take him. We better get going. It's been a long day."

It felt like there was so much more we needed to say to one another, but I didn't know where to start, so instead I just handed off Sam to Matt and walked him out to his truck.

"Thanks for everything today," I said as I held the door open and he belted Sam into the back seat, still half asleep.

"What are friends for?" He didn't quite look at me. "I'll catch you later?"

"Sure. Sounds good. Safe drive tomorrow."

🐾 🐾 🐾

My grandpa looked at me when I walked back in the door. "You okay?"

"As good as I can be." I joined him at the table. He and Sam had finally finished the puzzle. "I told Karen I'm not taking that job. I don't want to leave here. I know it might not work out, but I can't imagine going back there."

"You sure that's what you want?"

I nodded. "Absolutely."

"And what about Matt?"

"What about him?"

"Now that you're staying…."

"Grandpa." I shook my head. "Between you, Jamie, and Greta, I swear. I better make some calls. Let Trish's friends know we found her."

"I'll call Vick."

I winced. I knew the man needed to know that Trish was okay, but I really hoped for Sam's sake, and Trish's too for that matter, that when she woke up it was Jack by her side not Vick.

Jack had his issues. He certainly wasn't perfect. But I couldn't imagine Vick climbing into that canyon or staying by her side all those hours. Jack really cared for her. And for Sam. I just hoped Trish was smart enough to see it and to see that the life she could have with Jack was a lot better than the one she had with Vick.

CHAPTER 29

When I walked into the barkery the next morning Jamie wasn't singing. She wasn't even smiling. I should've called her the night before but I'd been so tired after everything that had happened. Plus, apologies like the one I needed to make are best made in person.

"Hey, Maggie. Wasn't sure you'd be in today."

I grimaced. "Sorry. About yesterday. About what a brat I was. You guys had really put a lot of thought into everything and it's such a great idea and…"

"We really do want you to be a part of it, you know. It won't be the same without you. And I'm sorry that…"

I help up my hand. "Wait. Just let me get this out, would you?"

She clearly wanted to keep talking, but she pressed her lips together and instead grabbed me a chocolate croissant and a Coke. (There's a reason she's my best friend. More than the fact that she's one of the few people in this world willing to put up with me.)

I laughed. "A bribe?"

"Maybe." She almost smiled.

Leave it to Jamie to feel bad about things when I was the one who'd been horrible.

"Look. You caught me by surprise yesterday. And I know you didn't mean it to be but it felt like you were all in on this secret and I wasn't. Which was hard. You're my best friend. And I'm losing you to Mason already and then..."

"But you aren't!"

"I know. That's just how it feels sometimes. You know how people get married and then disappear into their new married, coupled lives. So I took it poorly when you showed me those plans that were so well-developed and that I knew nothing about."

A Missing Mom and Mutt Munchies

"We didn't want to tell you if it fell through..."

"I know. I know you'd never hurt a fly. Which, thank God, because it's probably the only reason you're still my friend after all these years. Any sane person would've written me off long ago." She looked like she was going to object, so I just plowed ahead. "Anyway. Long and short of it is this. I was horrible yesterday. I'm sorry. And I told Karen I don't want to take that job. So, if you guys still want me, I'm in."

"You are?" She almost squealed she was so happy about it.

"I am."

"Yes." She hugged me and did a little jig around the café before launching into a non-stop discussion of all the ideas she had for the new resort.

I was able to finish both my Coke and the croissant before she finally stopped for a breath. "This is going to be so great, Maggie. Think of everything we can do with an entire pet resort!"

I was. And there were certainly some interesting possibilities. I still wasn't as sure as she was that everything would work out perfectly, but I was cautiously optimistic.

"As long as I don't have to wear heels," I told her.

She laughed. "Deal."

CHAPTER 30

Matt sent a few texts over the next couple of days keeping me updated on Trish's condition. She was in rough shape. Broken bones and lacerated organs. But having Jack and Sam there helped a lot. Matt decided to stay down there with them rather than come back home. I wondered why but I was too scared to actually ask.

Nothing had changed. He was still a great guy and I was still unable or unwilling to let him get any closer than he already had, no matter how I felt about him.

I was working at the barkery when Jack and Sam walked in.

"Hey, Maggie," Sam called, running over to say hi to Fancy.

"Hey, Sam. Hey, Jack. What brings you here?"

Sam answered for both of them. "We just came home to grab a bunch of stuff and then Jack and I are going to go back down to Denver to be with my mom. She's hooked up to all these machines all the time and her leg and her arm are in a cast and she's all bruised all over her face. But she was so happy to see us. And one of the nurses gave me this really cool truck. See? It lights up and everything."

"Nice."

I looked to Jack. "Where's Matt?"

"Home. We went there first to pack up some things and grab my truck. Sam and I are headed back to Denver now."

"Oh. Makes sense." I tried to hide my disappointment, but I'm not sure I did a good job of it. "You guys want some cake? Maybe a Coke to go along with it?"

"I'll take a coffee. Squirt here can have a milk, not a Coke. And just half a slice of cake. For both of us to split."

A Missing Mom and Mutt Munchies

Sam ran over and grabbed his hand. "Ah. Come on, Jack. Can't I have a whole slice?"

"No. You're hyper enough as is. Half a slice. And we're splitting it."

I joined them at the table by the window, taking the other half slice of cake for myself. "So what brought you in here today?"

"Business." Jack said. He looked at Sam. "Go ahead, buddy. It's yours to settle, not mine."

Sam dug into his backpack and brought out his piggy bank. "I wanted to pay you for finding my mom."

"You don't need to pay me, Sam. It's okay."

"Yes I do." He got that mulish look kids get right before they throw a loud temper tantrum.

"Really, Sam..."

He crossed his arms and glared at me. "I asked you to find my mom. I told you I'd pay you. You found her. So I'm going to pay you. Here."

He pushed the piggybank across the table at me, hard enough I had to stop it before it fell off the table.

I looked to Jack for help but he shook his head. "I'm with the kid. He hired you to find his mom and you deserve to be paid for services rendered."

The last thing I wanted to do was take the last twenty bucks from some poor kid for something I would've probably done for free. Although, offering to pay me had been a nice touch. That last little nudge I'd needed to listen to him. And it was good to teach him that services have value...

But, really. Twenty bucks.

I glanced at the piggybank and then at the very empty name-a-treat fundraiser jar. "Tell ya what. We'll compromise on this one. I'll take the money, but I'm putting it towards the fundraiser. Which means you've contributed the most to the fundraiser and you get to name my new dog treat. Deal?"

"Can I name it anything I want?"

A Missing Mom and Mutt Munchies

"Within reason. No cuss words. It can't be 'dog treat'. It has to have something to do with dogs. And I'd prefer if it be two words that use the same letters. Like Barkery Bites and Doggie Delights and Canine Crunchies. Other than that, it's up to you."

Sam narrowed his eyes at me as he thought about it, but then he nodded. "Deal."

"Okay, then. You let me know what name you come up with."

I left Jack and Sam to discuss their choices as I cleaned up a little on the café side. Jack came over to me as I was dipping a rag in a bleach bucket.

"There's another reason we came by," he said, keeping his voice quiet.

"What's that?"

He held out an envelope to me.

"What's this?" I dropped the rag back into the bucket and dried my hands off before taking hold of it.

"Matt asked me to mail this for him. It's been sitting on the kitchen counter unsigned for a week, but when we got home he signed it and put it in the envelope."

I glanced at the address. "He's going to re-enlist."

Jack nodded, watching me intently.

It was like a gut punch, but I didn't let it show. "Well, good for him. If that's what he wants to do, he'll be excellent at it. We need men like him, you know. This country."

"This town needs men like him."

"Jack..." I tried to hand him the envelope back, but he held his hands out to the side, refusing it.

"Since you're the reason he's leaving, you should mail it."

I opened my mouth to protest, but Sam came running over just then. "I have it. I have the name for the treat."

"Yeah?" I forced myself to smile. "And what is it?"

"Mutt Munchies."

"Mutt Munchies?" I could feel my eyes go wide with shock.

"Yep. Mutt Munchies." Sam didn't notice, he just grinned like it was the best name in the world.

A Missing Mom and Mutt Munchies

Jack laughed as I stood there, not sure what to say. I mean, Mutt Munchies? Really?

Of course, what did I expect leaving the name up to a young boy?

It was okay. Maybe not everyone would see it the way I had. Maybe it would seem perfectly normal to them. I sure hoped so, because there was no way around using it. Not with Sam looking at me that way. I wonder what Mason Maxwell was going to think of having a treat named Mutt Munchies in his new fancy pet resort.

Thinking of it that way...

"That's great, Sam. Mutt Munchies it is."

CHAPTER 31

As soon as Jack and Sam left, I did too. I needed to think. I wanted to be in Colorado. I wanted to be running a business with my best friend and spending time with my grandpa and with Fancy.

But without Matt...

I hadn't meant to let him become a part of my life. I hadn't wanted to fall for him. And yet, I had. Which meant I didn't want to lose him. I believe in serving your country and I'm proud of every man and woman who chooses to do so. But I'd be a fool to think that it doesn't come with risks. Or consequences.

I still firmly believed that Matt needed to make his own choices. That he couldn't choose to stay for

A Missing Mom and Mutt Munchies

me. It's not fair to ask that of someone.

But...

I didn't want to lose him. I'd walked away before. Turned my back on other men at other times. Chosen to stay on my path, alone. And yet with Matt, the loss was too big to bear.

I couldn't let him go that easy.

So I went to find him. I dropped Fancy off at the house and went to Matt's.

His truck was parked in front of his place, but he didn't answer when I knocked on the door. I peered through the windows I could reach, but no one was there.

I was about to leave when I heard the sound of a train and remembered the fishing spot he'd told me about. I looked around and found a faint path through the grass behind his place that led in the direction of the river.

I followed it as the train came closer, the breeze blowing my hair back and carrying with it that scent of water and freshness I always associate with Colorado.

Aleksa Baxter

He was seated on a folding chair—one of those ones with striped colored strips of plastic woven to form the back and seat, this one in red and white—his fishing rod propped in the mud at his side. An opened beer sat on top of an old cooler that could've probably fit a couple cases.

He couldn't hear me over the sound of the train.

I stood there, frozen, about ten feet away, watching as it passed. I didn't want him to leave but I didn't want to ask him to stay either. It was such a moment of vulnerability, such a moment of potential loss. Easier to turn and walk away before he saw me.

But then the train was past and I stepped forward. Matt glanced over his shoulder and gave me a nod, "Maggie. To what do I owe the pleasure? Have a beer. Have a seat." He reached into the cooler and held out a beer to me, keeping his own in his hand and gesturing towards the cooler which was the only other seating option available.

A Missing Mom and Mutt Munchies

I nodded towards where the train had disappeared. "I counted thirty-five cars," I said, taking the beer and sitting down facing him.

"You must've missed the first few. There were forty-two."

"Ah. Still not a record-breaker." I opened my beer and took a long sip. "Jack and Sam came by the store today on their way back to Denver."

"Really?"

"Sam wanted to pay me." I told him about Sam naming the new treat and we had a good laugh about it, but then lapsed into silence.

I stared at the river, not sure how to turn the conversation where it needed to go. Finally I decided the best way to deal with it was head on. I looked him in the eyes. "Don't go."

"What?"

I pulled the envelope Jack had given me out of my back pocket and ripped it in half. I figured worst case scenario he could always fill out new papers. "Jack gave these to me. Said you asked him to mail them for you. But I don't want you to go."

Matt frowned at me. "What...?"

Aleksa Baxter

"Look. Just listen would you? You have to stay. Jack is ten times more likely to stay on the straight and narrow with you around. And Trish and Sam need him. So you're helping there, too. And my grandpa's going to need your help next summer. And you're the best cop I know. And..."

I rushed on before he could stop me.

"And **I** need you to stay. This place won't be the same for me if you go."

Just saying it made me want to cry. I don't like to be vulnerable. I don't like to need people. Needing people means losing people and then hurting.

But if I couldn't be vulnerable in that moment to keep Matt then there was no hope for me. No one is actually perfect, but he was probably as close as you can get.

He just continued to stare at me so I rushed on. "I...Oh damn it. I think I love you, Matt. You can't go. Not when there's something here. You just can't."

I stood and started pacing, lost in my own thoughts. "I'm not a

A Missing Mom and Mutt Munchies

relationship person. I'm just...Not everyone can do that juggling thing where you let someone else in without smothering them or being lost in them. It's too easy for me to change when someone wants me to change. And there's so much I want to do that I'm not ready to be changed by someone else."

I stopped and frowned at him. He'd stood up and was staring at me. "Jack probably told you about Alex? About how he died?"

Matt nodded.

"But see, that's what no one gets. It wasn't him dying that broke me. It was realizing that his dying was probably the best thing that ever happened to me. That's what scared me away from relationships. I mean, I was going to give everything up for him. He wanted to move to Sweden to be a skydiving instructor and I was just going to go with him. I was almost done with college. I had plans of my own, but I was just going to walk away from everything I'd ever dreamed of being so he could pursue **his** dream. The only reason I didn't is because he died."

I crossed my arms tightly across my chest. "See, **that's** what love does to me. It sucks out who I am and replaces it with whoever the guy I'm with wants me to be. And I don't want that. But I can't lose you either."

Matt put his hands on either side of my face. "Maggie, I don't want you to be anyone other than you are, sharing plate for your dog, off-key singing, and prickly personality included. I'm pretty sure I love you, too. And I'm not going anywhere. I never was. I knew I was going to stay here the minute you decided to stay."

"What? But, Jack..."

Matt took one half of the torn up envelope and pulled out the blank piece of paper inside. "Jack knows how to get what he wants out of people. He played you."

"That..." (I called him a few words I won't repeat here.)

"I think we can forgive him just this once, don't you?" Matt smiled down at me as he brushed a piece of hair back from my face. I looked up,

A Missing Mom and Mutt Munchies

drowning in those blue eyes of his. Yeah, I could forgive him. Just this once.

Maybe.

And then...

Matt kissed me.

It was a good kiss. A **really** good kiss.

The type of kiss you want to be your last first kiss.

Oh yeah, I could definitely forgive Jack for this one.

EPILOGUE

It was my day off and I was finally going to have a chance to read that book I'd been dying to read for weeks. I grabbed myself a Coke from the fridge and went out back to join Fancy while it was still cool enough to read outside.

She was passed out on the grass at the base of the ramp, snoring quietly. I glanced over the rail to check on her, careful to keep from disturbing her, and had to keep myself from laughing when I noticed the tiny little bunny curled up against her tail, also sound asleep.

I desperately wanted to take a picture, but I knew that the minute I clicked on the camera option on my phone Fancy would wake up and the moment would be lost.

A Missing Mom and Mutt Munchies

Well, at least I knew she wasn't a stone-cold bunny killer after all...

Now to just hope that one little bunny wasn't the first of a hundred or else I'd be back to restraining my grandpa from "dealing with the situation".

I tell ya, the fun never ends.

If you'd like to spend a little more time with Maggie, Fancy, Matt, and the rest of the crew as they celebrate Halloween then check out **Halloween at the Baker Valley Barkery & Cafe**. Otherwise the next mystery novel in the series is **A Sabotaged Celebration and Salmon Snaps**.

ABOUT THE AUTHOR

When Aleksa Baxter decided to write what she loves it was a no-brainer to write a cozy mystery set in the mountains of Colorado where she grew up and starring a Newfie, Miss Fancypants, that is very much like her own Newfie, in both the good ways and the bad.

You can reach her at aleksabaxterwriter@gmail.com or on her website aleksabaxter.com

CPSIA information can be obtained
at www.ICGtesting.com
Printed in the USA
LVHW100318130422
716078LV00002B/40

Buffalo River Regional Library
Columbia, TN 38401